"I have a feeling about you, Mr. Long. I think you can help us."

"I think I understand, Miss Laura. Guess we'd better get back."

"Couldn't you wait just a while longer? My father has decided to camp in the cottonwoods for the night. Perhaps you could join us."

"Afraid not, Miss Laura."

"Don't make me . . ." she began softly, her hand plucking gently at his sleeve. "Don't make me have to ask you. Can you imagine what it has been like for me—and for my father—during this terrible trip—"

Before she could finish, Longarm turned her to him and kissed her on the lips. It was a long kiss, as sweet as spring water after an interminable thirst, and Longarm drank deep.

TABOR EVANS

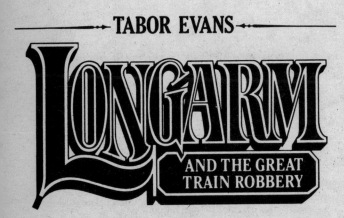

LONGARM

AND THE GREAT
TRAIN ROBBERY

A JOVE BOOK

LONGARM AND THE GREAT TRAIN ROBBERY

A Jove Book / published by arrangement with
the author

PRINTING HISTORY
Jove edition / July 1982

ISBN: 0-515-05602-2

Jove books are published by Jove Publications, Inc.,
200 Madison Avenue, New York, N.Y. 10016. The words
"A JOVE BOOK" and the "J" with sunburst are trademarks
belonging to Jove Publications, Inc.

LONGARM

AND THE GREAT
TRAIN ROBBERY

Prologue

As the Glendale train began its descent toward the long valley below, Finn Larson rose to his feet. At a glance from Seth Warner, the rest of the Warner gang got up, turned in a body, and left the rear coach, Finn Larson keeping to the rear, as planned.

As the gang walked quietly through the train, they left a man behind in each car, sitting casually, his back to the door, facing the passengers. There were only four coaches on this run, so that left Seth and Luke Warner to take care of the baggage car, with Finn stationed at their backs as they entered it.

Finn's lean face was almost hairless and tanned to a high gloss. His fair hair and eyebrows gave him a wide-eyed, innocent appearance—until you looked into his eyes. They were a pale, icy blue, as cold and cheerless as a winter sky. If there dwelt a soul behind those eyes, someone had once said of him, it was a damaged, twisted soul that was incapable of feeling genuine human emotion.

He wore a black, floppy-brimmed hat, a faded woolen shirt he had scrubbed clean himself, and faded Levi's. Two gunbelts sagged across his lean hips, and the walnut grips of both Colts gleamed immaculately. These two Peacemakers were the tools of his trade. Like any good craftsman, Finn kept them in excellent condition.

Finn Larson was happy. Any man is happy when he gets paid for what he likes best and Larson liked to rob trains. If he had to kill in the course of a robbery, he would. He liked that, too. So far, his ruthless willingness to cut down witnesses had prevented any description of him from reaching the Pinkertons, and that was just the way Finn wanted it.

Inside the coach next to the baggage car, Millie Dawson was looking out the window at the valley swinging into view below her. The vista was spectacular. For the first time since leaving Massachusetts, she felt her heart lift.

This was indeed lovely country, its breathtaking immensity so much more heartening than the constricted, grim landscapes of New England. Millie was sure she would have no difficulty teaching the children out here in this wide, expansive land, no matter what her father had told her. Children were children. They were the same everywhere—eager to learn, eager to search out the mysteries of the world about them. All one had to do was not sit on them or hound them into obedient little dwarfs, too frightened to respond—or laugh. Her own youth had taught her that.

And perhaps out here there would be someone . . .

She felt the tears on her cheeks and was shamed by them. Would she never forget that cad—or his senseless, brutal cruelty? Even worse, her awesome vulnerability to him. She had been putty in his hands.

2

Shuddering at the thought, she wiped her cheeks furtively with the back of her hand and glanced away from the window, aware suddenly that she was being watched by a portly gentlemen sitting across the aisle two seats up.

The drummer who was watching the girl touched the brim of his bowler hat in greeting and nodded pleasantly, just the trace of a smile on his round, porcine face.

The girl wasn't much to look at, he told himself, but then this part of the ride could get pretty damn dull. And she looked like she could use some company. He could tell she was from back East because of the milky, washed-out look of her. A mopey dishrag, she was more than likely coming out West in search of a man tall in the saddle and big enough and foolish enough to sweep her off her feet. If that was what she was hoping for, she was going to have a long, long wait—but maybe, in the meantime, he could liven things up for her just a bit.

But at his smile, the girl's pasty face went cold, her pinched nose rose a notch higher in distaste, and she looked quickly back out the window.

The drummer—his name was Ned Dudley—looked out the window himself and caught his own overblown countenance in its reflection. *Damn,* he thought bitterly, *who the hell are you kidding, Dudley? You got all the subtlety of a meat cleaver. She isn't much, that's true, but she already knows what you're after.*

Dudley sighed and watched the floor of the valley rush toward them. In spite of himself, he was impressed. The train was moving faster now that it was on the downgrade, while the immense, lowering rampart of the mountain they had just sliced through still cast its shadow over the train.

God, how he hated this constant traveling. He was damn glad this was his last trip. After this one, he was packing

3

it in. He would give his boy a home, finally. Be a real father to him at last. And maybe somewhere he would find a woman who wouldn't mind taking up with a widowed father and his half-grown boy.

Maybe. It was a thought. And it gave him hope. He stretched his legs and relaxed as he continued to look out the window, ignoring as best he could his pale, ghostly reflection in the glass.

Faith and Abe Wheatley had folded one of the seats back and were sitting facing each other, smiling. Josiah sat beside his father and Charity sat beside her mother. The brother and sister—ten and nine years old—were arguing about the number of telegraph poles that had stroked past since they went through the pass, their shrill, youthful voices piping pleasantly in the near empty coach. The youngsters were obviously having difficulty containing their excitement over this train ride.

But their father shushed them gently and settled the argument for them. "Four hundred and two," he pronounced solemnly. "That's how many telegraph poles."

"You sure, Pa?" Josiah asked.

His father messed Josiah's hair fondly with a work-calloused hand. "I'm sure enough, Josh. So now you'll have to find something else to devil your sister about."

"Aw, Pa!"

With a delightful squeal, Charity stuck her tongue out at Josh, then ducked her head into her mother's lap. "I won," she said. "I was closest!"

Watching the two youngsters was Jed Bigger, an old buffalo hunter sitting at the far end of the coach, in the seat nearest the door leading to the baggage car. Sitting across from him

4

was a man the buffalo hunter had thought might be fitting company for him on this long train ride.

But Jed had been wrong about that. The fellow across from him was a grim, unfriendly man who seemed content to stare out at the landscape. They were better than two hours out of Glendale and the fellow hadn't uttered a single word.

In the two hours since they'd settled into their seats, the old hunter had been studying the younger man. He could not help approving what he saw. The fellow was a lean, muscular giant with the body of a young athlete and a lived-in face. The hunter judged him to be on the comfortable side of forty, but too many suns and the cutting winds of winter had long since cured his rawboned features until they were as saddle-leather-brown as an Indian's. Only the gun-metal blue of his wide-set eyes and the tobacco-leaf color of his close-cropped hair and longhorn mustache gave evidence of his Anglo-Saxon birth.

Not that that mattered any to Jed Bigger. He had lived with Indians and Mexicans and Mormons. All men were decent if you gave them half a chance—and all men were pure-blooded devils when you gave them that chance, as well. He cleared his throat, in hopes he might be able to get a conversation going with his taciturn neighbor. But the man did not respond, continuing instead to stare grimly out at the landscape.

With a barely audible sigh, Jed grasped the barrel of his Sharps and glanced out the window at the valley floor beyond the tracks. As far as he could see was lush grassland. His old eyes looked in vain for the faint, tell-tale spot of buffalo. They were all gone now, every last one. At least from these hills.

But he had heard about the sizable herds still left in

5

Canada, and that was where he was heading. His pulse quickened at the thought and he gripped the barrel of his ancient rifle more tightly.

U.S. Deputy Marshal Custis Long turned from the window and smiled at the buffalo hunter. Then he reached into his inside pocket, took out two cheroots, and offered one to the man across from him.

Startled, the old hunter reached out quickly and took the cheroot. "Why, that's right kind of you, mister," he said.

"Thinking about the buffalo, I'll bet," Longarm remarked.

"I was," the old man admitted, brightening. He took out a pocket knife and sliced off the tip of the cheroot, then leaned forward as Longarm struck a sulfur match to life on his thumbnail and held it to the tip.

Leaning quickly back and puffing contentedly, the buffalo hunter said, "Time was when you could see buffalo wherever your eyes fell. Why, they was like autumn leaves covering the earth."

Longarm nodded to encourage the old hunter. His last mission had not been a pleasant one, and he was on his way to Tipton to report to the local county sheriff before returning to Denver. As the hunter spoke, the tension within Longarm eased.

This buffalo hunter had been places and seen things, and he knew how to tell a story. Smiling and nodding occasionally to keep the old man talking, Longarm settled back to listen...

Seth Warner, his brother Luke right beside him, bulled his way into the baggage car. It had taken a while for his insistent pounding on the locked door to arouse a response. As the two men, sixguns drawn, moved swiftly into the

6

baggage car, Finn Larson turned and hopped back across the swaying platform and reentered the coach they had just passed through.

He sat down in an empty seat, facing the passengers. There were eight people in the coach. The conductor, he knew, was in the next coach back. Finn glanced quickly around. A sodbuster and his wife and two yammering nits were on his side of the aisle. The next two passengers—a drummer on his right and a pinched-looking spinster sitting a few seats in front of him—seemed wrapped completely in their thoughts. They had not appeared to notice him or the Warners as they filed past on their way to the baggage car.

Across the aisle to his left sat an old hunter with a Sharps. He was puffing contentedly on a cheroot while he regaled a younger man sitting across from him with tales of the vanished buffalo. His listener seemed barely awake. The younger man, a tall, rangy fellow, was facing away from Finn, but Finn figured he'd better keep an eye on him when things started to blow. He looked big enough and quick enough to cause trouble.

An explosion from the baggage coach caused Finn to jump up, both Colts appearing in his long white hands even before he was fully upright. He knew at once what had happened. The Wells Fargo clerk had refused to open the safe—so Luke had blown it open, something they had hoped they would be able to avoid.

"Just sit easy," Finn said to the eight passengers, thumb-cocking both revolvers, "and you won't get hurt none."

The nester and his son swung around in their seat to stare at him, the boy peering at him over the back of the seat, eyes wide.

At that moment the door to the other end of the coach opened and the conductor hurried in, evidently drawn by

7

the sound of the explosion. He took one look at Finn standing in the aisle with both guns drawn and immediately pulled back, reaching into his coat for what Finn surmised was a small-caliber revolver. Finn fired from the hip.

The .45 slug caught the conductor high in the chest, slamming him back against the door. Yet the man seemed to have no sense. Even as he began to slide to the floor, he brought out a short-barreled Smith & Wesson. Finn took a full step forward, aimed carefully, and sent another round at the man. This one entered the man's head just above his nose, punching a neat black hole in his forehead and blowing out the back of his skull. A dark crimson stain blossomed on the door behind him.

The young woman screamed.

The sound of it was like a buzz saw cutting through Finn's eardrums. He swung his gun over to cover her. "Shut up, bitch!" he cried.

But the woman took one look at the cavernous muzzle pointing at her and began to scream even louder. Confused, furious, Finn aimed one of his Colts at her and squeezed the trigger. Her scream ended abruptly as the thunder of his third shot filled the car.

Finn became aware of movement beside him to his left. Glancing in that direction, he saw the crazy old hunter with the Sharps lurching to his feet. He was holding the long rifle over his head like a club. Finn fired into the old man's gut, knocking him back into his seat, his eyes bugging out in dismay as he felt the slug punch into his vitals.

The tall gent sitting across from him had drawn his Colt. Though he was knocked to one side when the old man was flung back, he managed to get off a shot. The slug whispered past Finn's right cheek. Before the tall gent could fire again, Finn pumped two shots into him.

But the old coot surprised him. Even with his gut hanging

8

out, he flung himself up at Finn and managed to get a grip on the barrel of the revolver in Finn's left hand. The old man's strength was startling. Unable to pull away, Finn clubbed down viciously at the man's skull with the barrel of his other, now empty, sixgun. His skull shattered, the old hunter fell back.

But now the tall sonofabitch was reaching for him. Finn swung around to deal with him, the bloodlust singing in his veins. Before he could fire at him again, however, an arm dropped about his neck and yanked him back. He gasped and felt whoever it was trying to grab hold of one of his sixguns. Swinging violently about, Finn flung his attacker off his back. The man crashed back into an empty seat.

It was the sodbuster.

Finn grinned. He hated nesters. They stank of cow shit. His father had been one in Minnesota, a shit-kicker who drank himself to an early grave with his own lousy moonshine, but not before he had beaten every one of his six kids almost daily with vicious, drunken thoroughness. As the suddenly terrified sodbuster backed up fearfully, Finn lifted the gun in his left hand and fired twice into the man, deliberately pumping the second round in low. The nester screamed and doubled over, clutching frantically at his crotch.

Turning back around to the two on his left, Finn saw that the tall gent was still game. He was reaching out for Finn, his eyes burning with hatred and cold fury. Steppling closer, Finn raised his empty Colt over his head and began to chop down viciously at the man's head and shoulders.

Longarm felt each blow dimly, as if it were happening to someone else. His chest was on fire and he saw the world through a red haze. All he wanted now was to get his hands about this mad dog's neck. Then he would die happy, drag-

9

ging the sonofabitch into hell with him.

Snatching at the gunman's forearm, he managed to swing up his right hand and catch his assailant about the back of his head. The man brought up his knee, hitting Longarm brutally in the chest. Longarm hung on, nevertheless, his left hand joining his right about the killer's neck. He began to squeeze then, his thumbs digging into the gunman's Adam's apple. Dimly he saw his assailant's eyes bug out as he dropped both guns and began tearing frantically at Longarm's tightening fingers.

That was when the train slammed to an abrupt halt, hurling both men sideways. The back of the seat caught Longarm. He lost his grip on the gunman, who went spawling into the aisle. Slipping down between the seats, Longarm saw the door swing open and two men push their way into the coach. They took one look at the carnage and swore in horror and dismay.

One of them helped the gunman to his feet anxiously. "Jesus Christ, Finn! What the hell you done here?"

"Never mind that," the fellow replied, massaging his tender neck. "The horses here yet?"

"What the hell do you think we stopped for?" the other cried.

"Let's go, then!"

From down the aisle came the sound of running feet. Three men passed Longarm's line of vision and disappeared with the others into the baggage car. Another one, not so fast, approached. As he hurried by his seat, Longarm reached out and tried to grab his boot. With a mean chuckle, the fellow pulled up, brought his foot back, and drove his boot deep into Longarm's side.

Longarm felt his insides expand into a dark flower of pain, and he went spinning into darkness . . .

Chapter 1

A month later, a gaunt, pale Longarm swept up Colfax and into the Denver Federal Courthouse, a rolled-up newspaper clutched in his hand. Elbowing his way unceremoniously through the throng of officious legal dudes, he strode swiftly up the marble staircase and pushed his way past the big oak door on which gold-leaf lettering proclaimed: UNITED STATES MARSHAL, FIRST DISTRICT COURT OF COLORADO.

The pink-cheeked clerk sitting before his newfangled typewriter machine barely had time to glance up as Longarm kept on resolutely past him and burst into Marshal Billy Vail's office. Vail, seated at his mahogany desk, glanced up with an annoyed expression on his face—until he saw who it was.

Jumping up, Vail reached out quickly to shake Longarm's hand. "Longarm!" he cried. "You're looking great! Just great! How long you been back on your feet?"

"Since I read this," Longarm growled, slumping into

Vail's red morocco leather chair. He opened the newspaper he was holding, leaned forward, and spread it out on the desk before Vail.

Sitting back down in his chair, Vail said, "Why, what's this?"

"Read it!" Longarm snapped. "The first column on the front page."

Vail did. When he had finished, his face wore an expression of profound disgust. "Jesus," he said softly. "Maybe I should have let you testify, after all. But you were so damn weak. And, hell, they had that drummer as a witness. And I thought they had the nester's wife, too."

Longarm took back the paper and read it once more, as if going over it a second time might possibly purge the fury that choked him.

WARNER GANG SET FREE

Buffalo, Wy., August 3—After less than an hour's deliberation, the jury returned to a crowded and hushed courtroom today and acquitted all six members of the notorious Warner gang of any complicity in the infamous Glendale train massacre.

The verdict was not remarkable, considering the manner in which the testimony of Ned Dudley was discredited by skilled attorneys for the defense. Also a factor was the refusal of Faith Wheatley, the widow of one of the victims, to testify. Speculation throughout the town was rife that the life of Widow Wheatley, along with that of her two children, had been threatened.

All members of the gang were promptly freed, with the exception of young Burt Williams, who is still being held by Sheriff Matt Simpson on a separate charge of horse-stealing. Williams was unable to post bond in the sum of $800 for his appearance at the next term of court and was returned to jail.

There has been some talk of transferring the prisoner to the more secure jail in Casper, so as to prevent his possible rescue by other members of the Warner gang. But Sheriff Simpson has assured all concerned that such precautions will not be necessary, as he plans on hiring a special guard to watch Williams.

Our sheriff is determined that one member, at least, of this lawless band shall not escape justice.

Longarm glanced bleakly up at Vail. "Damn it, Billy," he said. "I should have testified!"

"I know how you feel, Longarm. But there's nothing you can do about it now. The important thing is that you're on the mend."

"No. The important thing is to bring those animals to justice. Especially that murdering bastard they called Finn."

"Don't worry. They'll try something else and get strung up for it. They'll press their luck once too often."

"What makes you so sure of that? The way I look at it, they just got away with murder. They're going to lie low now and lick their wounds—and gloat. Hell, they might never surface again."

"They had their day in court, Longarm, and twelve of their peers saw fit to acquit them. That's it."

"No, it isn't."

Vail sighed wearily. "All right," he said. "All right. Have it your way. It isn't. Now, when do you think you'll be able to get back to work? I can give you local assignments for a while until you get your strength back."

"That's decent of you, Billy."

"You're a lucky man, Longarm. You could have died

from those wounds and the beating you took. I don't want to push your luck. Couldn't afford to lose my best man, could I?"

"Give me another week or two, Billy."

"That long?"

"That's all I should need."

Vail's eyes narrowed suddenly. Something in Longarm's expression alerted him. "What do you mean by that, Longarm? What the hell are you up to?"

"Unfinished business." As he spoke, he glanced at the paper in his lap.

Vail closed his eyes and leaned back in his chair. "Damn it, Longarm," the old lawman sighed wearily, "you know I can't allow you to do anything like that."

"You don't have to know about it."

"But you read what it said there. The members of the Warner gang were acquitted of all charges. You have no legal reason to go after them."

Longarm snorted derisively, then got slowly and carefully to his feet. "Two weeks, Billy. That's all I should need."

"Longarm, that gang almost killed you once."

"That's right. And they *did* kill a young woman schoolteacher, an old buffalo hunter, a farmer, and a conductor. Then they rode off with over ten thousand dollars in gold. Two weeks, Billy. That's all I'm asking."

Marshal Vail took a deep, unhappy breath. "If you go after them, it won't be official. I can't give you a warrant or anything. You'll be acting on your own. I wouldn't be able to back you."

"I know that. I'm not asking you to. All I'm asking for is the two weeks."

Unhappily, wearily, the old lawman shrugged his meaty shoulders. "All right then. Two weeks, but for God's sake,

14

be careful. I came near to losing you once."

Pausing at the door, Longarm looked back at Vail, a wan smile on his gaunt face. "Don't worry, Billy. I'm like a bad penny. I keep turning up."

Then he was gone. As the door closed behind him, Vail kept staring at the door, a deeply troubled look on his face. At last, reluctantly, he turned his attention back to the paperwork he had been busy with when Longarm burst in.

But he could not concentrate on the irksome form he was filling out. At last he gave up on it and, pushing himself erect, went to the window. He knew what was bothering him. He was wishing the impossible—that it was himself, not his best deputy marshal, who was setting out after the animals those fool jurors had set loose. But of course that was out of the question. He had gone to suet. The years behind this desk, years of pawing through the paper blizzard that kept blowing in from Washington, had sapped him, robbing him of the vigor Longarm still possessed—and the luck that went with it.

Vail caught sight of Longarm's tall figure moving off down Colfax.

"Good luck, Longarm," he whispered softly. "Get those bastards—but, damn your hide, keep that tail of yours down."

Sheriff Matt Simpson was about to open the door to his office and step out into the cool night to get a breath of fresh air when the door was yanked open on him and a tall stranger sagged drunkenly against the doorjamb. The stench of whiskey that entered with him was overpowering. If the sheriff had not reached out to grab him, the poor, besotted cowpoke would have collapsed.

Simpson helped the barely conscious man over to a bench along the wall. "Lonnie!" he cried. "Get out here!"

15

Stepping back, Simpson let the fellow sag back against the wall. He was a tall, somewhat gaunt drink of water with gunmetal-blue eyes and a longhorn mustache. He was sure as hell riding a high lonesome, yet there was something about him that didn't quite fit. Perhaps it was the clothes. They were too well cut—nothing an ordinary cowpoke would have had the sense to spend his money on.

"What the hell we got here?" Lonnie asked as he stepped out of the cell block and pulled the door shut behind him. "Another bagged cowboy?"

"Looks like it."

Lonnie chuckled. "Well, we sure as hell got the room."

The sheriff nodded. "At least the poor sonofabitch had sense enough to turn himself in."

"Probably don't have the price of a room."

"Lock him up, Lonnie. I'm going out for a breather."

Lonnie looked over the tall, broad-shouldered fellow sprawled on the bench. His head was resting back against the wall, his eyes closed, his mouth slack. An almost visible cloud of whiskey fumes hung over him.

With a weary shrug, Lonnie walked over and hauled the slack body to its feet. As he did so he glanced at the sheriff. "Remember, I'm off at ten."

"Don't worry," Simpson replied, "I'll be back in plenty of time. Just going to wet my whistle some. How's our star boarder?"

"Asleep. Jesus, Matt, it's sure lonely in there with no other prisoners."

"Yeah? Well, maybe this guy will liven things up," Simpson said as he stepped out the door.

Lonnie grunted as he pulled the drunk toward the cell block. The man was surprisingly heavy, he noticed, as he opened the door and pushed him in. There was sure nothing flabby about him. The poor sonofabitch had just been on

16

the trail too long, Lonnie figured sympathetically, remembering his own trail days—and town nights.

"In here, feller," Lonnie muttered, pulling a cell door open.

But, to his surprise, he was no longer supporting the stranger. The drunk had abruptly stepped back away from him. Lonnie glanced up and groaned. The inebriated cowboy was standing steadily before him, a sixgun held steadily in his hand, a cold glint in his eyes.

"Stand easy, Lonnie," the man said quietly, "and you won't get hurt. It's not you I'm after."

Reaching over quickly, he lifted Lonnie's sixgun out of his holster and stuck it in his belt, then snatched the key ring from his belt loop.

"Damn it, mister!" Lonnie cried. "You can't be goin' to free that horse thief! He's a killer—one of the Warner gang!"

The fellow stepped away from the cell and waggled his sixgun. "Get in there and shut up."

Unhappily and reluctantly, Lonnie stepped into the cell, his eyes riveted to the gun in the stranger's hand. Once inside, he turned about and watched through the bars as the fellow unlocked Burt Williams's cell and pulled it open.

"Let's go, Burt."

"Who the hell are you?"

"You got friends, mister. Now let's move it."

"Seth Warner? He sent you?"

"Let's go, damn it!"

Burt Williams did not argue any further as he hurried from the cell. Before he could leave the cell block, however, the stranger pulled him up short.

"Just hold it there a minute," he said, handing Burt Williams a handkerchief and a length of rawhide. As Williams took it, his rescuer said, "Get in there and gag this guard here. Then tie his hands behind him. And do a good job."

Lonnie groaned inwardly as Williams entered his cell. He knew for certain that Sheriff Simpson was not going to cut short his nightly visit to the saloon across the street, and that Lonnie would be trussed up like a turkey for close to four—maybe even five—hours. He started to pull back from Burt, but Williams grabbed him eagerly, stuffed his mouth with the silk handkerchief, then pulled his two hands roughly behind his back. It was obvious that Burt Williams was enjoying himself immensely.

Goddammit! Lonnie thought, his eyes swinging back to the tall galoot with the sixgun, *I should've suspected the sonofabitch. No matter how drunk he is, no cowboy's ready to turn himself in if he can still walk.*

By noon of the next day, after they had nearly exhausted their second relay of horses, Longarm turned north and headed into the high vastness of the Bighorns. He was sure that by this time they had effectively outdistanced any pursuit the local sheriff had been able to generate.

"Where are we heading now?" Burt Williams called to Longarm above the steady beat of their horses' hooves.

"Just ride, mister!" Longarm yelled back at him. "You'll know when you get there!"

There was no more conversation between them until Longarm pulled up at a narrow cleft in what had appeared to be a wall of rock. The cleft was hidden behind a tall boulder that seemed to have grown like some huge petrified plant out of the rocky ground.

"In through there," Longarm said to Williams. "I'll be right behind you."

The passageway was narrow and remained so for almost a quarter of a mile. Portions of the passage were so difficult to navigate that Williams had to be ordered on through by Longarm. At one point Williams's horse reared and almost threw its rider, but Longarm insisted that Williams press on.

At the last passageway widened. Soon they were riding over a wider trail. The sheer walls fell away and great, blessed patches of blue sky appeared overhead. A moment more and they were riding into a lush valley hemmed in on all sides by high, nearly perpendicular cliffs. Ahead of them, grassy slopes undulated lushly. There was the odor of pine in the air, and the smell, too, of ice-cold streams.

"Hey, this is some hideaway you got here!" Williams cried, gazing excitedly around him. "Sure beats the Hole in the Wall."

"Does it now?"

"Why, hell, man! You could hold off an army here."

Longarm just nodded as he led the way into the valley. After less than a mile, they rode up to a modest cabin built close to a cliff side and well into a grove of pine trees. A crude lean-to served as a stable.

As soon as they dismounted, Longarm walked over to fetch a spade that had been left leaning against the side of the stable and returned with it to Burt Williams.

"Take this," he said, handing the spade to him. "I'll see to the horses. There's a small rise on the other side of those pines, facing the valley. Pick a nice spot for yourself and start digging."

Williams looked at the shovel and then at Longarm, sudden panic showing in his face. "Dig?" he asked. "Dig for what?"

"Your grave."

"You must be loco, mister!" Williams gasped.

Longarm snapped the spade at the man. To prevent the shovel from smashing him in the face, Williams caught it.

"I told you," Longarm said coldly, "pick a spot and start digging!"

"I ain't crazy, mister! Why should I dig my own grave?"

Longarm smiled. "You already have. You dug it when you robbed the Glendale train. Hell, you're already a dead man."

"But, damn it, the Warners sent you to rescue me!"

"Did they?" Longarm smiled.

"Oh, my God," Williams groaned, as he took a step back. "Who the hell *are* you?"

"I was a passenger on the Glendale train when you and your boys robbed it, Williams. That jury was bought off, I suspicion, but there's no one with enough money to buy me off." Longarm drew his .44 and pointed it idly at Williams. "You going to start digging? Hell, I could just leave you out here in plain sight for the buzzards if that's what you want."

Williams stood for a moment holding the spade. Longarm thought he was going to cry. The outlaw had a round, weak face, a receding chin, and watery blue eyes. His carrot-colored hair was thinning, and there was a faint sprinkling of freckles across his forehead and cheekbones. He was a spineless dishrag, a species of human flotsam that could turn without qualm or hesitation into good or bad, depending on the whim, or the companions, of the moment.

When Lonnie had pushed him into the cell block back in Buffalo, Longarm had immediately recognized Williams. He was the last member of the gang to come running down the aisle of the train past him. It was this spineless no-account whose final, brutal kick had sent Longarm tumbling into oblivion.

Longarm pointed to the pines. "I can see you clearly from here. This valley is surrounded completely by steep canyon walls. You make a break for it and I'll cut you down."

Without a word, Burt Williams's shoulders sagged in defeat. He nodded and started toward the pines.

Williams was sitting on the edge of the grave, the handle of the spade resting on his right shoulder. Coming up behind him, Longarm glanced quickly around. Williams had picked a nice enough spot. There was a view of the entire valley from this pleasant prospect.

"See you got it dug," Longarm said.

Williams nodded without turning.

"I think we'd better mosey on back to the cabin and have something to eat."

"The condemned man ate a hearty meal. Is that it, mister?"

"That's about it."

"I'll stay right here, thank you."

"All right." Longarm reached across his belly and withdrew his .44. Williams looked up at him in sudden terror, beads of sweat standing out on his forehead.

"Never mind!" he cried, scrambling out of the grave. "Damn your eyes! I'll do as you say!"

Longarm slapped Williams hard. The force of it almost knocked the man back into his grave. "You're in no position to curse me, Williams," Longarm told him. "I reckon you better remember that."

Meekly, his hand up to his stinging cheek, Williams nodded.

After a meal of jerky, beans, and coffee, Longarm leaned back in his chair and looked across the table at Williams. For a condemned man, he *had* eaten heartily. Longarm

21

waited for Williams to speak.

"What now?" the man asked, glancing nervously up from his plate. Longarm could see the doubt and confusion in his watery eyes. He was finding it difficult to reconcile the meal Longarm had just provided for him with Longarm's stated intention of cold-bloodedly executing him.

Longarm shrugged. "I'm in no hurry. I don't much care for this sort of thing—not like your friends. It's a nasty business all around. That's how I look at it."

Hope sprang into Williams's eyes. He seemed pathetically eager to agree. "Why, that's just the way I see it," he proclaimed. "This *is* a nasty business, and that's the pure truth! Why don't you just let me go? I swear, you done punished me enough already, mister."

"No, I ain't. Not yet, I ain't."

Williams began to sweat. "Who the hell *are* you, anyway?"

"Name's Long. Custis Long. I'm a deputy U.S. marshal."

"And you was on that train, you say?"

Longarm smiled thinly. "Maybe you remember me. I reached out and tried to grab you as you went by. You kicked me in the side, as I recall."

Williams lost all the color in his face. "Oh, Christ! That was *you!* You got to believe me, Long—I didn't mean to hurt you none. I just didn't think. You was in my way and, besides, you didn't look like you was goin' to live!" He licked his dry lips. "Besides, Long, I been cleared of that Glendale robbery. Everyone in the gang was."

Longarm nodded. "I done some checking. You had the best attorneys that stolen money could buy, two gents named John Houk and C. L. Gates—and three of the jurors. That's why you were cleared, Williams—not because you or those dogs you ran with were innocent."

"How . . . how did you find that out?"

"I have my ways."

"Listen, we didn't get hardly nothin' from that robbery. The express only carried ten thousand we could use. The rest was in bonds."

Longarm nodded. "Your lawyers took the bonds. They had ways of cashing them. And they got almost face value for the lot. They and those three jurors were well paid."

"Well, damn it, you could have shown up at the trial. You could've testified. I didn't see you there."

"What good would it have done with three jurors already bought? Besides, I was in the hospital in Denver." Longarm leaned closer to Williams. "Tell me about the others, Williams. About Luke and Seth Warner. And Rob Turley and that woman of his, Wilma Reed. And Finn Larson. Tell me about that sonofabitch."

"It was Larson killed all them people, Long! You know that! It wasn't any of us. Finn, he always says the only way to get clear is to kill all the witnesses."

Longarm nodded, letting Williams run on. The stench of death was in the man's nostrils and he was ready—anxious, even—to spill his guts.

But as he rattled on almost steadily for the next half hour or so, it became obvious to Longarm that he knew precious little about Seth Warner and his brother or about Finn Larson. He was quite willing, however, to go on at some length about Turley and Wilma Reed.

Rob Turley was a Texan, and so was Wilma, his common-law wife. They came from Concho County, where Wilma had worked a small horse ranch for her mother. Williams, it seemed, had talked to her often about those early days in Texas. She dressed and forked a horse like a man, and always had, from as early as she could remember. It was these two who had met the train with the horses.

"And where might these two be now?" Longarm prodded.

Williams felt that Wilma and Turley would most likely be back in Texas now. About the rest of the gang, he could say nothing with any assurance, he insisted. He had no idea where Seth and Luke Warner had gone after the trial, and Finn Larson, he maintained, was a mystery of a man who disappeared after every job and only showed up a day or so before the next one.

When at last Longarm was certain that Williams had told him all he intended, Longarm stood up and looked across the table at him. "Time to go, Williams."

Williams looked up at Longarm, apprehension filling his eyes once again. The easy, relaxed way in which Longarm had questioned him, not to mention the meal, had given the man hope that this was just an elaborate hoax, that Longarm had only been trying to frighten him in order to get the information he needed. But now, as he looked once more into Longarm's eyes and caught their cold glint, he knew it was no hoax—that it had come time for him to die.

Silently, numbly, he got to his feet. Longarm indicated with a nod that Williams should precede him. Walking like a man in pain, Williams left the cabin and headed across the meadow toward the pines.

Longarm did not have to tell Williams where to go. As they passed through them, the pines echoed with the lovely, plaintive call of a hermit thrush, and Longarm saw the effect its melancholy song had on Williams. The outlaw seemed to wilt visibly.

Just before they got to the small ridge beyond the pines, Longarm unholstered his Colt. When they reached the gravesite, he nudged Williams in the back with it, pushing him toward the spade Williams had left in the grave.

24

"Better clean it out first," Longarm told him. "Some dirt's fallen back into it, looks like."

Williams took up the shovel reluctantly and set to work cleaning out the grave. Holstering his weapon, Longarm hunkered down beside Williams. Idly plucking a piece of grass, he began to chew on it, gazing abstractedly about him as he did so.

Longarm sensed the tightening in Williams's shoulders perhaps even before the man himself was aware of what he intended. As he shoveled, Williams lifted the spade a mite higher than usual. Bracing himself inwardly, Longarm continued to chew on the grass and look straight ahead.

Only when Longarm caught sight of the descending arc of the shovel's blade out of the corner of his eye did he allow himself to pull back slightly and raise his left arm to protect himself. He was fortunate the wooden handle rather than the blade struck his forearm. Rolling quickly back and away, he drew his sixgun. Williams started to follow him, the spade upraised, when Longarm fired. The round clanged off the blade, the force of the impact knocking the shovel from Williams's grasp.

Williams turned and fled toward the pines.

Remaining on the ground—as if he were still groggy from the blow he had suffered—Longarm aimed carefully and fired a second time, disintegrating a branch projecting just ahead of the fleeing man.

The shot added wings to his feet.

Slowly, carefully, Longarm got to his feet, listening to the sudden thunder of a horse's hooves as Williams galloped away from the cabin toward the valley's entrance. Rubbing his bruised left forearm, Longarm started to walk through the pines.

As he did so, a grizzled mountain man with a yellowing

25

beard that extended down to the second button on his red-checked woolen shirt stepped out of the trees and fell in beside him. He was carrying a long-barreled Kentucky rifle. Longarm had come to know Ike Santee long before he had become a deputy U.S. marshal, since both hailed originally from Longarm's home state, West-by-God-Virginia.

"You damn near let that foolish sonofabitch kill you," the mountain man commented. "I almost shot his ass off, but I remembered what you said and held back. By grannies, it wasn't easy. Now don't you think it's about time you told me why in hell you let that bastard get away?"

"Won't do no harm, I guess, Ike—since you were kind enough to let me use your place." Rubbing his forearm thoughtfully, Longarm paused on the edge of the pines. He could just barely make out the fleeing horseman. "By the time that gent finds the passageway out of here and works his way back through it, I'll be on the other side, waiting to follow. It's my hope he'll take me to the Warners."

Ike nodded sagely. "That's about what I figured. You scared the piss out of him, all right." Ike chuckled. "Yes sir, he oughta make fast tracks back to that rat pack, and you'll be right on his tail. You sure you don't want me to come along? Nothing I'd like better than to rest my sights on that bunch."

"No thanks, Ike. You've done enough. Like I said before, this is my party."

"Suit yourself, old son," Ike said.

Without any further discussion, Longarm started for his black. Ike was right. All Longarm had to do was to let this one rat lead him to his brothers. What Longarm would do once he cornered them was not entirely clear in his mind.

But one thing he knew for certain. He was not going to bring them in for another trial by jury.

26

Chapter 2

By noon three days later—well behind the tiny cloud of dust that was Burt Williams—Longarm pulled his black to a halt. He had glimpsed ahead of him the shadow of great hills lying vague and ominous upon the horizon. Towering over those foothills like protective older brothers were the massive, fabulous humps that made up the Absaroka Range. At the same time, Longarm caught the dim suggestion of a town huddled between two foothills. That must be Landusky.

Longarm had heard of the place. The silver that had given it birth had long since played out, turning it into a refuge for whatever scum the tides of misadventure washed its way—a perfect hole for the likes of Finn Larson and the Warner bunch to disappear into.

Longarm nudged his black forward. The afternoon sun burned like a slow brand on his back. At sight of a dry wash, he directed the black toward it, then let the animal

27

pick its way down the steep, gravelly slope. Once he reached the creek bed, the ridge behind him blocked the sun, giving him a welcome respite from the heat. He followed the creek bed for a quarter of a mile before easing his black up the other side of the steep bank. The moment he crested the bank, he saw just ahead of him a small Conestoga wagon halted beside a clump of willows. Its two-horse team was still hitched to it, and the horses were cropping the sparse grass at their feet.

Longarm saw the trouble at once. The wooden rim on the wagon's right rear wheel had shrunk in the dry heat of the afternoon, allowing the iron tire to fall off. A harried-looking fellow in his late forties was straining to lift the wagon so that a girl who appeared to be his daughter could pull the wheel off the axle. The girl was in her early twenties and was struggling mightily, but with little success, since her father was simply not able to lift the wagon high enough to enable the wheel to clear the ground.

Dismounting swiftly, Longarm grabbed a long dead branch he had spotted on the other side of the willows and fitted it snugly under the wagon's rear axle. The fellow who was trying to lift the wagon saw what Longarm was about, waited a moment, then nodded to him and, straining might-ily, heaved upward. At the same time, Longarm lifted his lever—and that made the difference. The wagon lifted and the wheel turned freely. The girl tugged on it frantically until it dropped off the axle and slapped down into the dust.

Slowly Longarm allowed the wagon to settle back until the axle was resting on the ground. Then he stepped back, breathing heavily.

"Name's Bill Miller," the man said, thrusting out his hand. "And this here's my daughter, Laura. Much obliged, mister."

Longarm shook the man's hand. "Custis Long," he said.

28

"Pleased to meet you." He touched the brim of his hat and smiled at Laura. "You too, ma'am."

Miller took a handkerchief out of his rear pocket and mopped his brow. He was a heavy, graying man a little under six feet tall. His seamed face was weathered and tanned. It had the texture of a face whose owner spent a lot of time following a plow.

His daughter had a touch of flame in her dark hair and hazel eyes that were appraising Longarm somewhat coolly at the moment. Her face was open and good to look upon, but she was not pretty. She was better than that. She was handsome in a completely feminine way. Though she was dressed in Levi's and a cotton shirt and wore heavy men's boots, her masculine attire could not hide for an instant how much of a woman she was. Indeed, to Longarm, the straining shirt and hip-hugging Levi's were more of an assault upon his senses than any frilly, lace-trimmed frock.

"I thought I was going to drop that wagon before Laura could get the rim off," Miller said, grinning ruefully at Longarm. "You sure came along at the right time."

Longarm looked down at the wheel. "You'll need to find a water hole to soak that rim in," he said.

"That's what I figured," Miller said.

Longarm glanced back the way he had come. "There might be one farther on down that dry creek bed. I caught a glimpse of cottonwoods. They looked green enough."

Miller said nothing as he glanced around at his two horses. He would have to unhitch one of them and ride it bareback to the cottonwoods, carrying the wooden rim and the tire. Once he found the water hole—assuming it was there—he would have to refit the tire to the rim, then soak them both in the water until the wood swelled enough to lock the tire back onto it.

Reading his thoughts, Longarm said, "No need to unhitch

your horses." He turned back to his own horse and swung into the saddle. "Hand me the wheel and tire."

As Miller did so, Laura said, "You'll need help hanging on to them."

Longarm clutched at both of them and grinned down at her. "Looks like I will. Got any ideas?"

"Yes."

She swung up behind Longarm and snaked one hand about his waist, then thrust her other arm through the iron tire. Clasping her hands together, she hugged Longarm snugly, trapping the tire within the circle of her arms. Longarm put his own arm through the heavier wooden rim and set off.

As Longarm had surmised, the cottonwoods enclosed a deep, spring-fed water hole. Laura was a great help in finding a rock of the right heft to knock the iron tire back onto the wheel's rim. They worked together without much conversation and then rolled the tire into the shallowest portion of the water hole. Finished with that portion of the task, they found a shady spot under one of the cottonwoods and sat down to wait for the water to do its work.

"You were a real help, Laura," Longarm said. He had soaked his handkerchief in the water and was now mopping the perspiration off his face with it.

"Thank you," Laura said.

Despite the exertion of a few moments before, Longarm noted, she appeared as cool and unruffled as the wild flowers that ringed the water hole. And just as attractive.

"Where are you and your father bound, Laura? Landusky?"

"No, to the Deer River country beyond it. We have kin in those parts and Pa is going to settle on a quarter section there."

"I see. Just the two of you?"

"My mother is dead. And . . . and we're hoping my sister will join us, if she finds out we're here."

That sounded somewhat strange, but Longarm did not pry. He simply nodded.

"The last letter we got from her was four years ago," Laura volunteered, obviously deeply troubled and anxious to confide in someone. "It came from Landusky. The man she had run off with had deserted her when the mine played out."

"Four years? That's a long time in these parts."

The girl nodded unhappily and looked away from Longarm at the submerged wagon wheel. "I know. But one of those kin of ours—my uncle—wrote and told us he had seen her in Landusky a year ago. He just caught a glimpse of her on the street. So it looks like Ellen may still be in the area."

"Ellen?"

"Yes. She's a year older than me, but people say we look more like twins than sisters."

"I sure hope you find her, Miss Laura."

Laura looked into Longarm's eyes. "And what are you doing in this land, Mr. Long?"

"Landusky is a rat hole. There's some rats in there I'd like to flush."

"Are you a lawman?"

Longarm nodded. "But I'm not on official business this trip."

"I see," she said. She looked at him for a moment as if she were trying to decide whether she could trust him. Then she said, "Look at me closely, Mr. Long, and remember what I look like."

Longarm smiled. "That's not very difficult."

Ignoring the compliment, she said, "If you come upon a woman who resembles me, Mr. Long, would you please

31

get in touch with my father or me?"

"Of course. That's a promise."

She smiled in sudden relief and leaned her head back against the tree. "Good," she said. "I have a feeling about you, Mr. Long. I think you can help us. Alone, I don't see how my father and I could ever find Ellen—and I know how desperate he is to find her. He loves me, Mr. Long. But since Ellen ran off, he's been a very unhappy man—and I have been without my closest companion. I said people mistook us for twins. Well, sometimes I had the odd feeling we *were* twins. That's how close Ellen and I were."

"I think I understand, Miss Laura."

Longarm got to his feet and approached the water hole. The wooden rim had expanded enough to lock the iron tire snugly against the rim. Reaching down into the water, he pulled the wheel back up onto the grass. After a quick inspection, he saw that the wheel was now in fine shape.

"Guess we'd better get back," he told Laura.

She was standing very close to him. "Does that mean you'll be riding into Landusky tonight?"

"The sooner I get there, the sooner I'll find those rats, I'm looking for," he replied.

"Are you so anxious to deal with scum?"

"It's something I have to do, Miss Laura."

"I can understand that," Laura said. "But couldn't it wait just a while longer? My father has decided to camp in the cottonwoods for the night. Perhaps you could join us."

"Afraid not, Miss Laura."

"Don't make me . . ." she began softly, her hand plucking gently at his sleeve. "Don't make me have to ask you. Can you imagine what it has been like for me—and for my father—during this terrible trip? You are so strong. I feel so safe around you. I want to feel your arms about me . . . I need to . . ." She turned quickly away. "Oh, dear God, what

32

am I saying? You'll think I'm—"

Before she could finish, Longarm turned her to him and kissed her on the lips. It was a long kiss, as sweet as spring water after an interminable thirst, and Longarm drank deep.

"I'll camp for a while beyond the cottonwoods, a dry camp," he told her softly, his arms still about her. "Visit me when you can."

Then he kissed her again.

She arrived with the moon. It cast a sheen over her slim figure and imparted a shimmering corona to the thick abundance of her hair. Remaining as silent as the night about her, she let her long nightgown fall to the ground, stepped out of it, then knelt beside him. He opened his soogan for her. She slipped in beside his own waiting nakedness and fitted her long lovely warmth against him as he took her face in both his hands and kissed her on the lips.

She moaned softly and drew herself still closer to him. Reaching down, she touched him and uttered a tiny cry of delight as she felt how large he had grown. In a burst of passion, she pushed him down and mounted him swiftly, enclosing his engorged shaft with an almost savage downward thrust.

She was going too fast for him, much too fast, but the fiery warmth of her charged him with an answering excitement, and a delight that was intoxicating swarmed up from his loins. Still thrusting, she fell forward onto him, her breasts crushing onto his chest, her lips devouring his. As he began to buck upward, her tongue began to work in a devilish mimicking of his own frantic thrusts.

Out of consideration for his partners, Longarm usually did what he could to delay his climax. But this time it was out of his control. He could muster no restraint at all as he bucked wildly. She hung on, uttering a low, continuous

33

squeal of delight. His climax came in a fierce, headlong rush that emptied him completely, deliciously. But she had not climaxed and refused to release him.

To his delight, he found himself growing once again within her. She squealed softly and flung herself up and back, her fingernails digging into his thighs. The pain from her frantic, scrabbling fingernails aroused him to a second passionate peak. Watching her in wonderment, he saw her luxuriant hair flaring wildly, framing her flower of a face in its dark penumbra. She was grimacing with the urgency of her need by this time, and despite the wetness of her, she managed to enclose his resurgent erection with a tenacity that ignited him.

Caught up once again, he flung her over onto her back, remaining deep within her all the while and continuing his powerful thrusting without missing a beat. Her sudden cry of delight told him this was precisely what she wanted. She leaned back, hurling her pelvis upward to meet his savage thrusts. At last she grew rigid, flung her arms about Longarm's neck, and pulled him convulsively down upon her, all the while uttering a piercing cry.

Aroused now beyond anything he had experienced in a long time, Longarm lifted her buttocks with his big, rough hands and continued to slam down into her. With another cry of delight, she flung her legs up and about him, her lips still fastened to his. He could smell the hot musk of her desire in her eager, panting breath. It had an amazing effect on him—and on her as well as she swept toward another climax.

By now both of them had become pure, unbridled passion—lust incarnate, released at last from all fetters...

Later, clean of urgency, Longarm watched Laura's pale, moonlit figure disappear in the direction of her father's camp. Then he turned to his black and stepped up into his saddle.

After a few minutes' ride, he crested a moonlit ridge and caught sight of Landusky in the distance. Taking one last look in the direction Laura had taken, he gently spurred his mount on toward Landusky's dim cluster of lights.

Chapter 3

Well before sundown that same day Seth Warner looked up from his poker game and saw Burt Williams pushing his way through the Silver Slipper's batwings. He cursed bitterly and slammed his cards down, ignoring the startled looks of the other players.

Seth and his brother Luke had purchased the Silver Slipper with their share of the take from the Glendale train robbery. What they wanted now above all else was the chance to enjoy the fruits of that notorious massacre in relative peace.

That was why Seth Warner was so furious at Burt Williams's unexpected and unwanted presence. They had disbanded the gang and intended never to bring it together again. Now here was this stupid sonofabitch, big as life and twice as ugly, striding into the Silver Slipper.

As Seth watched, seething, Burt Williams caught sight of Luke behind the bar. At once Williams pasted a smile on his face and hurried toward Luke like a puppy heading for its mother.

Luke appeared to be as surprised as Seth. He put down the glass he was polishing and greeted Burt. Seth left the poker game and hurried up to the bar. Doing his best to hide his anger, he slapped Burt heartily on the back.

"Burt, you sly old sonofabitch!" he cried. "If you ain't a sight for sore eyes! Last I heard, you was in the lockup in Buffalo."

"Well, I ain't there now. I got sprung."

"How'd you manage that?"

"You won't believe it when I tell you."

"Try us," said Luke, slapping a shot glass down in front of Burt and filling it with whiskey.

"It's a long story," Burt said, tossing down the drink and shoving the empty glass toward Luke for a refill. "Right now, all I want is a place to hole up."

Luke filled Burt's glass again and cleared his throat. "How did you find us, Burt?"

"I heard you talking at the trial."

As Luke flung his brother a furious glance, Burt smirked. "No sense in blaming Seth," he said. "Neither of you fellows knew I was close enough to hear what you was saying. I kept my ears open on purpose—in case I ever needed help later on."

"And you need help now?" Seth asked carefully.

"You bet I do. And so will you when you hear what I got to tell you."

"Let's step over here where we can talk, Burt," said Seth, taking Burt by the shoulder and pulling him gently toward a small table against the wall. Luke called an assistant from the office to tend the bar and joined them, bringing a bottle and three glasses to the table. As the three sat down, Luke spoke first.

"All right, now, Burt," he said. "Let's have it. What's this you come all the way up here to tell us?"

Burt started with his escape from the Buffalo jail, described the fellow who engineered it, then finished up with his near death at the man's hands.

"I'm lucky to be alive," Burt concluded. "This feller was plumb clear out of his mind. But he was dead serious, and that's a fact." He shook his head and shuddered. "That sure ain't no pleasant thing, I can tell you—looking down into your own grave that way."

Luke and Seth exchanged glances. "Just how bad did you hurt this feller with that shovel?" Seth asked.

"I don't know. I didn't hang around to find out."

"Then you don't know if he was hurt bad or not," Luke prompted carefully. "That right?"

"I told you, I was too busy runnin' from the crazy sonofabitch!"

"So you don't know if he followed you here," said Seth. "Is that right, Burt?"

At once Burt caught their drift. Glancing quickly from one to the other, he came alive to his danger. "I didn't say that. And now that I think of it, I'm pretty damn sure I wasn't followed. And when he asked about you and Finn, I told him nothing he could use."

"He was after Finn, too, was he?" Luke asked.

Burt nodded.

"And us," said Seth. "He's after us, too. Ain't that right, Burt?"

"Hell, he's after *all* of us!"

"You say he told you who he was?"

"Yeah. Custis Long. He's a U.S. deputy marshal."

Seth leaned back suddenly, staring furiously at Burt. "Goddammit, Burt! That man who let you out of that jail was *Longarm!* I've heard of him. Ain't *you* never heard of him?"

"Longarm?" Burt looked unhappily from one face to the

39

other. "Why, hell! Sure I heard of him. I just never connected his name with that lawman, is all. Jesus! No wonder! But, hell, what he done wasn't legal! He broke me out of that jail all by hisself, and he even locked up that deputy who was guarding me."

"And he was on that train, you said?" Luke asked, staring intently at Burt.

Burt nodded miserably.

"He must be the one Finn told us about," Seth said to his brother. "The long drink of water that gave him such a fight."

Both men turned their cold gaze on Burt Williams. Their friendliness had vanished completely. Burt looked pleadingly at Luke. Of the two brothers, Luke was the one Burt had always turned to when he needed help.

"I need a place to hole up, Luke," Burt told him. "Soon's I figure out what to do I'll light out. I promise. I won't bother either of you any more. Just give me a place to hole up for now, is all."

Luke reached over and patted Burt on the wrist. "Don't you fret none, Burt. We'll give you a place. We not only bought this here saloon, but the hotel next door."

Seth smiled. "Hell, Burt, you came to the right town if you want a place to hide out. Don't you worry none about that." He leaned closer. "Thing is, Burt, we got new names now. You might say as how we're turnin' over a new leaf. No more robbing trains and such like. We was lucky to get free of that last job and it sure cost us dear. We don't aim to push our luck. So while you're here, you gotta be sure you don't let on who we are."

"Sure," Burt said eagerly. "Don't you worry none about that. I won't say a word. You know you can trust me. What's your names now?"

Seth grinned. "Luke here is Tom and I'm Jim Bronson. Figure we could still be brothers, long as we changed our names."

Burt moistened dry lips. "Sure, Seth—I mean, Jim. Hell, you can trust me not to say nothin'."

"I knew we could, Burt," said Luke, leaning back in his chair and regarding Burt in a friendlier way. "We don't need to worry none about you, and that's a fact."

"You see," said Seth patiently, as if he were addressing a not-too-bright child, "we want to put that train robbery behind us. We don't want the stink of it to follow us here."

Luke poured Burt another drink. Burt threw it down as quickly as he had the others. Studying him carefully, Seth realized that Burt was almost out on his feet. As the man stood up, he staggered slightly.

Reaching out gently, Seth urged Burt to sit back down. "Just what did you tell Longarm, Burt?"

"Like I said—nothing about you. And when he asked about Rob and Wilma, I told him they were back in Texas."

"How the hell do you know they *didn't* go back to Texas?" Seth demanded angrily.

Burt's face went pale at Seth's display of anger. He shrugged desperately. "I was just guessing, is all."

"Like hell you were. You know they're up here, too."

Burt pushed himself to his feet. "I'm tired," he said. "Bone tired. I had a long ride today. You gonna show me a room, Luke?"

"Why, sure, Burt. You look plumb tuckered out." Luke pushed himself to his feet. "Just follow me."

As Seth watched his brother escort Burt from the saloon, the anger he felt was mixed with dismay. He swore furiously under his breath and in utter frustration ran his big right palm down over his face. It had not been easy for him to keep his composure with that spineless milksop sitting so close to him.

He and his brother were already settling nicely into the business of running the saloon and hotel. The profits were not all that great, but it was a living. Luke was putting on weight, becoming jowly, and he had a gut that was already beginning to fold over his belt. But that was Luke's problem. Seth prided himself on remaining as lean as a sapling—and found great pleasure in presiding over a daily poker game in the rear of the saloon. At times, his winnings were quite gratifying.

It had been a fine idea to buy this saloon and settle down. It was about time he and his brother did something sensible for a change. And in a way, they had Finn Larson to thank for it. Finn's cold-blooded ruthlessness during the Glendale train robbery had turned the entire country against them. It had taken close to ten thousand dollars to save them from its consequences. The James gang were heroes—but not the Warner gang. After what Finn had done, robbing trains was no longer a profitable lark for the Warner bunch—and maybe that was just as well.

So all that was behind them now—as long as no one found out who they were. Here in Landusky they had new identities, and though it was a tough, hardscrabble town, Seth had never known a place that didn't need a watering hole of one kind or another for its resident hardcases. And as sure as hell burns, no one ever got poor providing an outlet for men's vices.

Seth was about to pour himself another drink when a shadow fell over his table. He looked up and found himself staring into Finn Larson's ice-cold blue eyes.

"You saw him, did you, Finn?" Seth asked bleakly.

"I saw him," Finn said, slumping into the chair Luke had vacated. "I was watching from the other side of the room. How in hell did he find you?"

"The sonofabitch kept his ears open at the trial, seems like. He's a real snoop. It was my fault. You know how I bragged about this place—my ace in the hole."

Finn nodded bleakly. "Yeah, I remember. But I didn't think Williams had heard."

"Neither did I."

"So now what? How come he's in our hair?"

"He's scared, Finn. He's runnin' from someone." Seth paused and glanced significantly at Finn. "You remember that buzzard you said had you around the throat during the train robbery?"

Finn's icy eyes came to life with interest and he leaned forward. "I remember," he said. "What about him?"

"Well, you didn't kill him, and he's a deputy U.S. marshal. Long is his name."

"Long?" Finn frowned and sat back in his chair.

Seth nodded grimly. "That's right—the one they call Longarm."

Finn swore softly. Then he smiled, and the smile sent an icy chill up Seth's spine.

"And to think I almost killed the bastard," Finn remarked. "Hell, maybe what they say about the sonofabitch is right. Maybe he *is* indestructible."

"Well, I sure as hell ain't anxious to find out, Finn— one way or the other."

Finn's eyes narrowed. "You saying Longarm might still be on Burt's tail?"

"That's what I'm thinkin'. Course, I can't be sure of it. And Williams says it ain't so. But how the hell can you trust him to tell it straight? The way I see it, he was too busy pissin' in his pants to notice if he was bein' followed or not. The thing is, he got away from Longarm too damned easy, I'd say."

"You're goin' too fast for me, damn it," Finn said in sudden exasperation. "Last thing I knew, Burt was in the lockup in Buffalo. Tell me what he told you—all of it."

Seth repeated Burt's story almost word for word. When he finished, Finn nodded thoughtfully. "I think you're right, Seth. Longarm scared Burt plumb loco, then set him loose. Sure as bears shit in the woods, he's on that dumb bastard's trail right now." Finn looked around the saloon nervously. "Longarm never got a look at you or Luke. But he sure as hell will remember my face. Looks like I'll be moving out tonight."

"Now, look here, Finn. You know as well as I do that as long as Burt Williams is alive, none of us are safe."

Finn gazed coldly at Seth for a moment or two, then nodded his head slightly. "I guess you're right, at that."

Seth smiled and drove his point home. "By the way, Finn, how's that girl you bought from Ma working out?"

"A hell cat," Finn replied appreciatively. "But she'll calm down. Only not too much, I hope. I like to take it from them when they ain't so anxious to give it." Finn smiled.

Seth shuddered inwardly. He felt a bit sorry for that woman. "All right then. You're all set in those mountains somewhere with that girl, and me and Luke have a deal in this town. But with that stupid sonofabitch Burt Williams on the loose, there's a good chance we'll lose what we got. You wouldn't want that, would you?"

"All right. Spit it out, Seth. What you got in mind?"

"We got to do something about Burt Williams."

"You don't mean we, Seth. You mean me. It's time for old Finn Larson to do your dirty work for you. Ain't that what you mean?"

Seth shrugged nervously. "Hell, Finn, you just know more about that sort of thing."

Finn chuckled coldly. "Sure I do, and that's a fact. You don't like Finn when he does things to rouse the newspapers and the Pinkertons, but you sure as hell like to have him around to clean up the messes you and your brother leave behind. Ain't that so, Seth?"

Seth stirred uncomfortably under Finn's cold gaze. "Damnit, Finn! You goin' to help out or not?"

"All right, I'll take care of Williams. I never did like that whelp, anyway. But this is it. I'm staying out there after this. I've got me a woman who'll make me a fine squaw when I get her housebroke. There's good fish in the stream, plenty of beaver to trap, and the hunting's good. The hell with this place. The hell with towns. And people. They ain't none of them worth a shit."

Finn's words had been spoken in a quiet, deceptively soft monotone. Yet the ingrained bitterness they revealed was not lost on Seth, who knew that he was sitting across from the most dangerous animal on earth—a human killer.

To cover his nervousness, Seth poured himself another drink. He would be as glad to see Finn leave this town for his hideaway as Finn would be to go. And if he never came back, that would still be too soon for Seth.

"Just one thing, Finn," Seth managed, tossing down his whiskey. "Do it as neat and quiet as you can, will you?"

"Sure. I'll do it quiet." He reached for the bottle of whiskey Seth had been pouring from. "You got any rat poison, maybe?"

"Poison?"

"You heard me. Arsenic would do just fine."

Seth was startled. The idea was so simple it was perfect. "Luke's got some out back, I'm pretty sure. He's been using it on the rats in the hotel cellar."

45

"Go get some as soon as Luke gets back. A couple of shot glasses full should be enough. Bring it to me here. Then maybe I'll just pay Burt a vist. He looked like he could use a drink. I'll tell him this bottle is on you—compliments of the house."

He smiled then. Seth looked away from the terrible, soulless eyes and got hastily to his feet. As he left the table, he saw Finn lift the whiskey bottle to pour himself a fresh shot. It was the same bottle, Seth had no doubt, that he would soon be offering to Burt Williams.

Burt Williams stirred fitfully, then sat up. Cold sweat was standing out on his forehead and he could feel his heart beating frantically. Sick, disordered traces of a nightmare still clung to him. He looked blearily around the dingy room, peering fearfully into the shadows.

There was a sharp knock on his door. He took a deep, grateful breath. It must have been an earlier knock that had awakened him. He swung his feet off the bed and walked to the door.

Sudden caution made him pause before it. He leaned his ear against the upper panel. "Who is it?" he called softly.

"Got a bottle for you, Burt," came a familiar voice. "Luke said you might be needing it."

It was Finn Larson, Burt realized with a shudder. But the news of the bottle was enough. If there was one thing he needed right then, it was a drink. Burt pulled open the door and stepped back.

Grateful though Burt was for the liquor, the sight of Finn Larson striding into his room unsettled him. He would have been a lot happier if Luke or his brother—or anyone but Finn Larson—had brought him the bottle. The slim, fair-haired killer with the icy blue eyes had always been able to fill Burt with fear. And this time was no exception, even though Finn managed to quiet Burt's misgivings some when he smiled and handed Burt the bottle of whiskey.

Taking the bottle gratefully, Burt closed the door behind Finn, then slumped eagerly on the bed. Uncorking the bottle, he drank from it greedily, his Adam's apple doing a quick jig.

"Whew!" he cried, wiping his mouth off with the back of his hand. "That was just what I needed."

"Don't be a hog, Burt," Finn said, pulling up a chair and sitting down backwards in it, his crossed arms resting on its back. He took a shot glass out of his pocket and held it out to Burt. "Share the wealth. It's the best Luke has. He told me so himself."

"Oh, sure, Finn," Burt cried hastily, resting the neck of the bottle on the rim of Finn's shot glass and pouring. "Sure!"

After filling Finn's glass, Burt took another swig from the bottle. As the whiskey burned its way into his gut, he felt his spirits lifting. He looked boldly at Finn Larson. "I suppose you want to hear about that lawman who sprung me. That right, Finn?"

"Sure, Burt. Tell me about him."

"He was a big, mean sonofabitch, that's for sure. Looked part Indian, and that's a fact. And he sprung me neat enough. Only he was crazy, I swear! He made me dig my own grave and was going to shoot me in cold blood. But I showed the sonofabitch. I broke loose of him. Hit him with the shovel, I did. Knocked him on his ass." He snickered nervously and took another swig from the bottle. "I sure was lucky to get away from that man, I tell you."

"Yes, you were, Burt. You purely were."

Burt saw that Finn had not yet finished his glass. "Drink up, Finn," he said, aware that his words were not coming as clearly as before and that with each passing second his head seemed to be spinning faster.

"Sure," said Finn. But he made no move to drink the whiskey.

Burt's lips were getting numb and he was having difficulty controlling his tongue, but he managed to speak anyway. "You gonna hole up in this town with us, Finn?"

"Not on your life," Finn snapped. "This town stinks. It stinks of people." Finn glanced out the window at the dark shoulder of a mountain peak leaning ominously over the town. An early full moon was sitting just above it, sending its soft glow into the room. "I got me a place up there— away from the stench of towns and people."

Burt was beginning to feel sick to his stomach. Nevertheless, he took another hefty swig. "That's right, Finn," he said recklessly. "I know all about you. After a job you go off up there and hide in your hole like a rat!" He grinned foolishly. He was so far gone he didn't even care if he got Finn Larson mad. He sure was riding a high lonesome.

Slowly, deliberately, Finn got to his feet and lifted the chair he was sitting in and placed it back down in the corner where he had found it. Then he walked back over to Burt and stood looking down at him. He still held the shot glass of whiskey in his hand. He hadn't touched a drop.

Holding the full glass out to Burt, he said, "Here. Drink up. I never could stand cheap whiskey."

Burt took the glass, gazed up at Finn in confusion for a moment, then shrugged and threw the shot down his throat. "Ain't cheap whiskey, Finn," he said, handing the glass back. "You said so yourself—Luke's best goods." He belched noisily and immediately felt worse.

He shook his head. He sure as hell was beginning to feel rotten. A fierce headache had exploded inside his skull and the room seemed to be moving around him. Glancing over to the window, he was surprised to see that it was not open. Where was that cold wind coming from? A sudden, bone-deep chill had fallen over him. Deciding on another drink, he noticed that his hand shook as he lifted the bottle to his mouth and drank deeply.

Wiping his mouth with the back of his hand, he almost lost his balance and fell off the edge of the bed. He sure as hell was getting drunk, all right. Really soused. But there was a queer, metallic taste in his mouth. He reached for the bottle again, hoping the whiskey would wash away the taste. But before he could bring the bottle back up to his mouth, a sudden, excruciating cramp deep in his gut caused him to double up. He almost dropped the bottle.

Finn was smiling. Reaching out, he took the bottle from Burt. Then he grabbed a fistful of Burt's hair, yanked the man's head back, and brought up the bottle. Poking the neck of the bottle recklessly past Burt's teeth, he emptied its contents down his throat. As Burt frantically gulped down the fiery liquid, he looked past the bottle at Finn's face and at Finn's malevolent eyes. They were alight with triumph.

In that terrible instant, Burt knew the truth.

Finn was poisoning him!

With a strangled cry, Burt flung Finn away from him. But Finn remained on his feet easily, then moved close to Burt again, eyeing him with cold, alert interest, as if Burt were some insect he had just impaled on a pin.

"What's the matter, Burt?" Finn asked, his voice laced with mockery. "Feeling a mite poorly, are you?"

With a despairing groan, Burt tried to get up. He was desperate to get out of this room and away from Finn. He needed a doctor. His stomach was on fire. But his arms and feet were enormously heavy, like lead. And no matter how desperately he tried to hurry, his limbs responded with excruciating slowness. He looked down at his feet. They seemed miles from his head, as if they were no longer a part of him.

Yet, somehow, he managed to push himself erect. For a moment he teetered dangerously, then took a step and, with a muffled cry, collapsed forward onto the floor. The moment he hit, he doubled up, his arms wrapped about his flaming abdomen, aware with a kind of sick horror that he was going to defecate where he sat. He closed his eyes and groaned in a mixture of terror and shame as the stench of his own excrement assaulted him. He was so cold—so damn cold! The pain in his gut increased and his teeth began to chatter so hard he could no longer keep them clenched.

Oh, Jesus! Sweet Jesus! He was going to die!

Finn stepped away from Williams's twitching body and, with the bottle of whiskey in his hand, left the room. Moving silently down the hotel stairs, he waited until the desk clerk went back into the office, then slipped across the small lobby and out into the night. His horse was behind the general store along with his two packhorses, both of which were already loaded and ready to go. He was glad. All of a sudden he was anxious to rid himself of the stench of death and get back to that woman of his.

Turning into the alley behind the store, Finn hurled the empty whiskey bottle into a dark corner and heard it smash sullenly against a wall. He smiled and kept on toward his waiting horses. The one they called Longarm would come to a dead end here in Landusky—and that dead end would be Burt Williams.

Which meant Finn would not have to worry about that lawman's iron fingers closing once more about his throat. Finn had made his last trip back to Landusky—but it had been an interesting trip, at that.

Chapter 4

Longarm rode into Landusky and down its main street past single-story frame and log buildings. His way was lit by lantern light glowing dimly through open doorways and dust-coated windows. It was late, but there was still activity centered about the single intersection. Reaching it, Longarm noted a large wood-frame building housing a general store and a large saloon that called itself the Silver Slipper. Next to it sat a dilapidated two-story hotel.

The livery stable was across the street from the Silver Slipper. As Longarm rode up to it, the figure of the hostler materialized out of the gloom of its entrance. The man took the black's bridle as Longarm dismounted.

"Second stall back," the hostler said.

Longarm nodded and led his black into the stable. After removing the saddle, he stood for a moment with his hand resting on the horse's sweaty back, then slung his saddlebags and bedroll over his shoulder, snaked his Winchester from its scabbard, and left the livery. For a moment he stood in the dark, sizing up the mean cluster of buildings that remained of Landusky. Then he squared his shoulders and started across the street.

He could hear clearly the boisterous shouts punctuated by the click of poker chips that swept out through the batwings of the Silver Slipper as he walked on past it to the hotel. After registering, Longarm fixed the slightly built desk clerk with his uncompromising stare and asked him if his good friend Burt Williams had arrived yet.

"Mr. Williams?" the clerk repeated nervously.

"I didn't see his name on the register," Longarm said, smiling deceptively. "But he should be here by now. This is the only hotel in Landusky, ain't it?"

"Sure. That's right. This is the only hotel."

"Burt rode in earlier this afternoon. He's got red hair— what there is of it." Longarm smiled, his eyes burning into the clerk's. "Which room is he in?"

"Oh...yes!" The clerk swallowed nervously. "The gentleman with the red hair? He's in room eight. On the second floor."

Longarm smiled. "If he's here, why didn't my friend register?"

"He didn't need to," the clerk answered hastily. "Tom Bronson brung him over here personal. He told me to give your friend a room on the house."

"That so?"

"Yes sir, that's what he told me, so that's what I done."

"Well, that was real white of Mr. Bronson, wasn't it?"

"Yes sir," the clerk replied nervously, aware that Longarm was being sarcastic. He was beginning to perspire some.

Longarm picked up his key and headed for the stairs, glancing back at the desk clerk as he started up them. "Thanks," he said. "And don't bother to tell my friend I'm here. I want it to be a surprise." There was more than a

52

hint of steel in Longarm's voice.

The clerk's round head bobbed anxiously on his narrow neck. "Of course, sir."

Longarm continued on up the stairs. Before entering his own room, he paused outside room eight and placed his head against the door. He caught the sound of someone breathing heavily, almost gasping. Maybe Williams was having bad dreams. Longarm walked back down the hallway to his own room, unlocked his door, and went inside.

The room smelled of dust. He dropped his gear on the bed, leaned his Winchester against the wall close by it, then slipped out of his brown coat. Unbuckling his supple leather gunbelt, he hung it over the bedpost at the head of the bed. Just to be on the safe side, he withdrew his double-action Colt .44–40 from its holster. He checked the firing pin carefully, then spun the cylinder a couple of times. He'd traveled through a lot of dust this past week, and he wanted to be sure his weapon was ready.

Draped across his vest was a gold watch chain. He lifted the Ingersoll watch from his left breast pocket. To the other end of the chain was clipped the small but deadly weapon that served as a watch fob: a twin-barreled .44 derringer.

Examining the powerful little pistol quickly, he took it over to the low dresser and placed it and the watch carefully down upon it. Then he took off his vest and rolled up his shirtsleeves. Untying his shoestring tie, he poured some tepid water from the pitcher sitting on the washstand into the waiting bowl and bent his face to it, washing the coating of alkali dust off his face and neck with his bare hands. A rough muslin cloth had been hung on a hook on the side of the washstand. He used it to dig the sand out of his eyes and to dry himself. This meager toilet was a poor substitute for a bath, but it would have to do for now, he realized, as he straightened and looked out the window.

The dark street below was pocked with occasional patches of yellow light flaring dimly from the windows and doors of the saloon and the hotel. Across the street, alongside the livery stable, a small restaurant called Bim's Place was still open.

Longarm was not hungry. Bill Miller's gratitude for his help had been matched by generous hospitality. But Longarm could use a cup of coffee, and while he drank it, the restaurant window would give him a clear view of the saloon. If Burt Williams woke up and went looking for his friends, Longarm would see it all from the restaurant.

Re-arming himself quickly, he shrugged into his coat, clapped on his snuff-brown Stetson, and left the room.

As Longarm entered the tiny restaurant, he surprised the owner, who was approaching the door, obviously with the intention of locking it. But Longarm shouldered his way resolutely into the place and headed for a table by the window, and the owner—a short, squat fellow—shrugged wearily and followed him.

"Just a cup of coffee," Longarm told the man.

With a barely audible sigh, Bim disappeared into the kitchen. Longarm leaned back and looked out the window at the Silver Slipper across the street. It occurred to him that if the place didn't quiet down some, he would have some difficulty getting any sleep that night. The men he saw entering and leaving comprised a colorful assortment of bewhiskered, dust-laden gunslicks, miners, and assorted drifters. They were a boisterous crew that undoubtedly had been drawn to this town not despite its isolation and lack of prosperity but precisely because of it. In short, Landusky was the perfect place for the Warners and the other members of their gang to lose themselves.

Bim brought Longarm a steaming mug of black coffee. Longarm paid the owner and sipped the scalding coffee, studying the sign over the saloon's entrance. In the lower right-hand corner of the sadly worn sign, the name of the former proprietor had been clumsily scraped off and the names of its new owners, Jim and Tom Bronson, painted over it. The paint looked fresh.

Longarm turned around to look for Bim. The restaurant owner was leaning against the kitchen doorjamb, his arms folded, his gaze fixed balefully on his sole customer.

"Looks like the Silver Slipper has new owners," Longarm said.

Bim had a toothpick in his mouth. He shifted it from one corner of his mouth to the other. "Yeah."

"For how long?"

"Two, three weeks, maybe."

"Newcomers to town?"

Bim studied Longarm carefully. Then he straightened up and took the toothpick out of his mouth. "Who the hell ain't newcomers to this town? You got a reason for asking all these questions, mister?"

"You're goddamn right I got a reason, Bim," Longarm said. He smiled. "You got any more coffee in that pot?"

Bim disappeared back into his kitchen, came out with a pot of coffee, and poured a second cup for Longarm. "That's your last cup, mister," he said. "I'm closin' up."

He left Longarm and a moment later the lawman could hear the man cleaning up in the kitchen. He was not being as quiet as he might have been. Longarm smiled to himself and continued to look out the window at the Silver Slipper.

He had hoped that he might be lucky enought to catch sight of Burt Williams leaving the hotel and entering the saloon for a nightcap. If he could catch Williams talking to the owners of the Silver Slipper that would clinch it. But, hell, he already had enough. One of the new owners—Tom Bronson, he called himself—had just taken it upon himself to give his old gang member a room in his hotel, free of charge.

Longarm nodded decisively. Perhaps now was the time to reel in his bait. He would return to the hotel and reintroduce himself to Burt Williams. At the sight of Longarm, Williams would be only too willing to lead him to Finn Larson and the other gang members, Longarm had little doubt.

A hand came down on Longarm's shoulder. Startled, Longarm turned swiftly, his right hand snaking under his frock coat and closing about the grip of his .44. Bim ducked back quickly.

"Hey, listen, mister," the man cried, "I told you! I gotta close up now. I don't usually stay open this late as it is. And, hell, you're just settin' there."

Longarm released his hold on his .44 and held up his palm to Bim. "Ease off there, Bim," Longarm told him quietly. "You made your point. Been riding too far between lights, looks like. Lost track of time."

Longarm got up, settled his snuff-brown Stetson down more firmly on his head, and left the place.

Crossing the street, he reentered the hotel. The desk clerk was asleep in his cubbyhole of an office, the sound of his snoring coming clearly to Longarm as he mounted the stairs to the second floor. Approaching the door to Burt's room, Longarm removed his Colt from its holster and prepared to rap on the door. When Burt answered, Longarm planned to move swiftly back down the hallway to his room and disappear inside. If Burt was still nervous, this mysterious knock should send him scurrying for help—straight into the arms of the other gang members.

Longarm rapped sharply on the door with the barrel of his revolver and waited.

There was no response—or was there? Leaning his head closer to the door, he held his breath so he could hear more clearly. Yes. There it was again—a kind of gurgling cry. Or was it a moan?

Longarm stepped away from the door and knocked a second time, louder. This time he was sure. There was someone on the other side of the door—someone who was dragging himself across the floor toward it. Lifting his foot, Longarm kicked at the door. The flimsy panel splintered and the door swung into the room, slamming to a halt against the inside wall.

By the dim light of the single kerosene lamp on the wall behind him, Longarm glimsed Burt Williams doggedly inching his way closer to the door, one hand reaching out like a claw. Stepping into the room, Longarm was immediately assailed by the stench that came from the man. He had soiled himself.

Longarm knelt by him. Williams lifted his head and squinted painfully at Longarm. Pain blazed out of the man's eyes. He grimaced in agony and tried to say something, but all that came out was a strangled gasp.

"What is it, Williams?" Longarm asked. "You're pretty damn sick, looks like."

Williams shook his head convulsively. "Ain't sick," he managed. "Poisoned! I been poisoned!"

"Who did it?"

"Finn . . ."

"Larson? Finn Larson?"

Williams nodded his head frantically, then began to shake all over. Longarm could see perspiration standing out clearly on his waxen forehead. The shaking grew more violent. It was obvious that Burt Williams was just about at the end of his rope. The convulsions grew stronger. His face went

57

almost blue as he reached out and grabbed Longarm's wrist to hang on to, his mouth working painfully as he tried to talk.

Longarm leaned closer despite the stench. "Where's Larson?"

Williams's crazed eyes stared out the window past Longarm. "Out there ... mountains ..."

Longarm swung around to look out the window. Over the town hung a great, lowering peak, the leanest and tallest of the Absarokas. If Finn was out there somewhere, holed up among those peaks, it would be a cold day in hell before Longarm tracked him.

Williams's teeth began to chatter loudly. Longarm looked back at the man and stood up. Burt Williams would soon be a dead man. There was nothing Longarm could do for him, but if there was a doctor in town, Longarm felt he might as well get hold of him.

"I'm going for a doctor," Longarm told him.

"Save ... yourself the trouble," Williams managed. "I'm done for ... already. Get them for me ... the bastards!"

"The Warners?"

"Yes! Get 'em!"

"Where are they?"

"Down ... stairs," Williams gasped.

That was all the dying man could get out. He tried to speak again, but all he could do was clutch his bowels more tightly and utter a long, continuous moan. The pain, Longarm realized, must have been excruciating.

Abruptly, Williams's lean frame grew rigid. A kind of peace passed over him. He closed his eyes and seemed to sigh. Then his body settled into the floor as the stench that hung over him like a curse became suddenly sharper. Longarm's stomach heaved sickeningly. He backed up hastily and left, pulling the splintered door shut behind him before he went down the stairs.

Longarm stepped out through the open hotel doorway and paused a moment to suck into his lungs the clean, sharp air sweeping down off the peaks of the Absarokas. There was a touch of pine in it, mixed with the faint chill of snow. It went a long way toward clearing out the stench of death that still clung to his nostrils.

He stepped off the board walk and crossed the street to the livery. The hostler was cleaning a stall in back by the smoky light of a coal-oil lamp. When the man saw Longarm approaching, he seemed relieved. The horse manure was heavy and from the looks of his leathery face, he was an old, not very strong ex-puncher who didn't take easily to this kind of town labor. Leaning his pitchfork back against the stall, he thumbed his floppy-brimmed hat back off his head and stepped out of the stall.

"You be wantin' your hoss now, mister?"

Longarm shook his head. "I'm wondering if maybe a friend of mine already left. He was a thin fellow, sandy-haired, clean-shaven."

The old cowpoke looked shrewdly at Longarm. "You sound like a lawman, mister. Or maybe you're a bounty hunter."

"I asked you a question," Longarm said coldly. "You fixin' to answer me or not?"

The cowpoke sighed. He was not all that interested in crossing Longarm. "No one like the feller you described left from this here livery."

"From *this* livery, you say."

"Yup." There was an obstinate twinkle in the old man's eyes. "From this livery stable."

Patiently, Longarm said, "You mean you saw this gent

ride out of town, but he didn't leave from here."

The hostler nodded. "You got it, mister. Feller like you described. Had his own horse along with two packhorses out back of the general store. Them packhorses was pretty well loaded up." The hostler looked shrewdly at Longarm. "Fact is, he left not too long afore you rode in—only he rode out the other way, headin' straight for North Pass. You just missed him."

"Thanks," Longarm said wearily. "Now, would you tell me where I might find the town constable—or the sheriff?"

"We ain't got neither, mister. Not in this town. It eats lawmen alive, it does."

"Do you have an undertaker—or a doctor?"

"We got both, mister. The barber does our buryin'. His name's Steep, Millford Steep."

"And the doctor. Where can I find him?"

"Doc Beaufort takes care of Ma Ridley's whores." He spat a heavy wad of chewing tobacco to the straw-littered floor. "He ain't good for much, I hear. Seems like it's the girls who take care of him."

"Where's Ma Ridley's place?"

"First house down the next street." There was a twinkle in the hostler's eyes again. "You can't miss it. Ma likes to advertise. She favors red curtains and has the best piano player in the territory, I hear tell."

"Never found out for yourself?"

"I'm a stove-up cowpoke, mister. But, stove-up or not, I never paid for it in my life, and I ain't a-goin' to start now."

"Thanks," Longarm told the hostler and left.

Ma Ridley seemed very pleased to greet Longarm. She pulled the door open and stepped back, a wide grin on her heavily-rouged face.

"Why, come right on in, mister," she cried. "Let me have your hat and coat. Why, you look big enough to take on two of my girls at once. And that's the God's truth!" She slapped her heavy thighs and laughed heartily at her ribald suggestion.

Longarm stepped inside. Ma closed the door behind him as two scantily clad women appeared in the inner doorway. All the lampshades in the place were either pink or red, and scarlet drapes were at all the windows. The piano player the hostler had mentioned was out of sight somewhere pounding away on an upright.

"It's not entertainment I want," Longarm told Ma Ridley, removing his hat. "I understand there's a doctor on the premises."

"A doctor? You mean Doc Beaufort?"

"If that's his name."

"There's been a shooting, has there? Funny—I didn't hear a thing."

"No, ma'am," Longarm replied as patiently as he could. "There hasn't been any shooting. Could you send someone for the doctor?"

Ma Ridley turned to one of the two girls. "Stella!" she cried, her voice suddenly harsh. The transformation was startling. "Wake up that sot! Tell him he's got a patient."

The taller of the two, a stringy, unhappy-looking girl who looked as if she had been very poorly used, headed past them and up the stairs. Ma Ridley looked back at Longarm, the affability of a moment before having vanished completely. She was wearing a dark maroon gown that started well off her shoulders and didn't get too serious about covering her until it was a few inches above the nipples of her broad bosom. A little more than five feet tall, she must have weighed at least two hundred pounds. She was holding a red satin fan in the pudgy, beringed fingers

61

of her right hand. Stepping back from Longarm, she began fanning herself swiftly, her doughy, rouged face cold. "You new in town, mister?"

"Yes, ma'am."

Her eyes narrowed. "You with them two what bought the Silver Slipper?"

"Now, who would they be, ma'am?"

"The Bronsons—Jim and Tom."

"That what they're calling themselves now?"

"You mean you don't know them?"

"Heard about them, and that's about it. You don't like them?"

"Don't like anyone who calls Finn Larson their friend."

Longarm smiled. "Neither do I, Ma."

She relaxed and was about to paste her welcoming smile back onto her face when the girl she had sent upstairs for the doctor hurried down the stairs. Glancing up the stairwell behind her, Longarm saw a tall, handsome, but cadaverous man in a clean white silk shirt and immaculate black frock coat and pants descending the stairs. He had a leather bag in his left hand and a well-kept, shiny black leather holster at his hip.

He paused halfway down the stairs and began to cough, hastily thrusting a handkerchief up to his mouth. He leaned against the bannister for support. As he gave himself up to the coughing, his entire frame shuddered convulsively. He was a lunger, Longarm realized, come West in search of a cure, more than likely.

The doctor's spasm of coughing gradually subsided. He pushed himself away from the bannister, pocketed his handkerchief, and continued on down the stairs as casually as if there had been no interruption at all.

"Doctor Lemuel T. Beaufort at your service, sir," he

said, extending a long, pale hand out to Longarm. "What seems to be the trouble?"

Longarm introduced himself and shook the doctor's hand. He found his grip to be surprisingly strong. "A friend of mine has been poisoned," Longarm told the doctor. "He's in the hotel—room eight."

"I suggest we hurry," the doctor said, brushing past Longarm and pulling the door open.

Longarm followed the doctor outside and joined him on the street. "There's no need for you to hurry," he told the man. "I'm pretty sure he's dead by now."

The doctor pulled up and turned to contemplate Longarm with some irritation. "Then why, may I ask, have you seen fit to disturb my . . . evening in this fashion?"

"I would like you to determine if my suspicions are correct, that he has indeed been poisoned—and, if possible, by what."

"Does it really matter?" the doctor asked wearily.

"It does to me," Longarm replied.

"Is this official business, Mr. Long?"

"Yes," Longarm admitted. "I'm a lawman."

"And the victim is not really your friend."

"No, he isn't."

With a shrug, the doctor started up again. "All right," he said. "But I warn you, my fee will be double."

The desk clerk awoke at their entry a few moments later and scurried out from behind his desk when he saw the doctor. He followed them up the stairs, uttering plaintive queries all the while. Longarm ignored him, and when he pushed open the door to Williams's room and turned to let the doctor in, he saw the clerk turn and bolt back down the hallway, his hand over his mouth.

Longarm lit the lantern on the dresser while the doctor

put his bag down beside Williams and proceeded to examine him, noting the dead man's curved position, the arms hugging the abdomen.

"He was convulsing, looks like," the doctor said. "And incontinent. Yes, it could be poison. Arsenic, maybe. A good stiff dose—but he didn't die very quickly."

Longarm picked up a shot glass from the dresser. There was a small trace of whiskey left in it. Handing the glass to the doctor, he said, "Maybe there's something in here."

The doctor stood up and sniffed the glass. "Whiskey, all right—and you're right, there's a trace of something else. Could be arsenic, but there's no way I can tell for sure. I don't have what I'd need to make a proper analysis—not in this town." He shrugged and handed the glass back to Longarm. "But what does it matter? The man's dead. Poisoned. That's the beginning and the end of it, I'm afraid. It could be a suicide, you know."

"I don't think so," said Longarm. He glanced quickly around the room. There was no whiskey bottle in sight. Not on the floor or on the dresser. He bent quickly to look under the bed. Nothing. The dead man emptied a bottle of whiskey laced with arsenic into his gut, left the glass in plain sight, and caused the bottle to evaporate into thin air. Not likely.

"I think I'll go downstairs and visit the Silver Slipper," said Beaufort, coughing slightly, his handkerchief at his mouth. "After this, I need a drink. The new owners of this hotel will have to bear the expense of this man's burial, I'm afraid—unless, of course, they want to leave the corpse right here." The doctor smiled thinly as he tucked his handkerchief away. "I'd better go down and inform them."

"Good idea," said Longarm. "I'll join you."

* * *

64

Seth Warner was studying his hand intently, his poker face showing no emotion at all. But that didn't mean a thing. A grim elation was building within him. He had just drawn a pair of tens, and that gave him two pair, aces and tens. It was about time, he thought. Up until now the cards had been going against him with a frequency that had made him doubt he would ever win another pot.

Two other players folded. The cowpoke sitting across from him tossed another twenty into the pot, then leaned back, content. Seth looked back at his hand. Damn it to hell! The cowpoke had asked the dealer for two cards. Could the sonofabitch have a full house?

Seth was about to match the twenty and raise it another twenty when he glanced up and caught sight of the hotel desk clerk bolting into the saloon, a look of pure, naked terror on his pale face. As Seth watched, the clerk reached across the bar and grabbed Luke with both hands.

"Someone's dead upstairs!" the clerk cried shrilly. "That fellow who was just in here! The one you gave a free room to! He's dead!"

Seth slapped his hand down onto the table and jumped out of his seat. The sudden movement caused the neat stacks of chips in front of him to spill forward across the table.

"I'm out!" he barked to the other players as he hurried over to the bar.

Grabbing the desk clerk by the vest, he spun him around. "Now, what's all this?" he demanded. "Who's dead?"

"That redhead! The one Mr. Bronson brought over to the hotel!"

"What happened to him?"

"I . . . I don't know! He was lying there—smelling awful!"

"Apoplexy, more'n likely," Seth snapped.

"Or drunk," suggested Luke. "Sometimes a man'll drink

himself into the grave if he does it on an empty stomach."

"More'n likely that's what it was," said Seth, nodding sagely, trying to calm the clerk.

By this time a crowd had gathered around them. The saloon's patrons were hanging on every word.

"How did you happen to find him?" asked Seth.

"I didn't. His friend did."

"His friend?"

The clerk nodded quickly. "He went for Doc Beaufort."

Seth did not want to believe what he was hearing. "Now, you hold it right there," he said to the clerk carefully. "You say the dead man was not alone—he had a friend?"

The clerk nodded quickly. "That's right, Mr. Bronson. He rode in after dark. He said he didn't want me to disturb Mr. Williams. Said he wanted to surprise him."

"Thanks, Willy," said Luke, lifting the gate and coming out from behind the bar. "We'll handle this now. You just get back to that desk and stay there."

"Yes sir, Mr. Bronson. But what about the body?"

"Never mind that. Just get back to the front desk.."

As Seth watched the clerk scuttle hastily from the saloon, he saw Doc Beaufort and a tall, grim-looking fellow with a longhorn mustache enter the saloon. Seth's heart grew cold. The tall drink of water was looking straight at him and Luke—like he knew just who he and his brother were and was mighty glad to find them.

It was that lawman, all right—the one they called Longarm. There could be no doubt about it. Seth swore bitterly to himself. He should have known. That yellow-belly Williams could not have taken even the most casual precautions for that lawman to have ridden in this close on his tail. The sonofabitch must have been riding practically within sight of Williams all the way. Burt had probably never even looked back once.

"Bronson!" Doc Beaufort called out. "You got a stiff in room eight. I suggest you haul it out of there soon as you can get him buried. He stinks something awful."

"I just heard," said Seth, moistening his suddenly dry lips. "How'd you happen to get there so fast, Beaufort?"

"Meet Custis Long," the doc said, indicating his companion with a nod of his head. "He's a deputy U.S. marshal. He's the one who discovered the body and he decided I'd better have a look."

"Nice of him," said Luke.

The moment Beaufort introduced the tall stranger as a deputy U.S. marshal, the patrons who had gathered about Seth and the clerk began to evaporate swiftly, like ground fog struck by a shaft of sunlight. More than half the men in this town were running from something, Seth realized, and they were suddenly more than a little anxious to find a quiet table where they could keep their heads down and bide their time. A few of them were already drifting out of the saloon.

"Drinks on the house for you, Doc," said Seth, "and for your friend, too."

The doc nodded his thanks and Luke moved back behind the bar. "What'll it be?" he asked.

"Rum," said Beaufort.

"Whiskey," said the lawman. "That is, if I dare."

Luke paused with the bottle of whiskey in his hand. "What's that supposed to mean, mister?"

"That fellow up in room eight was drinking whiskey that must have come from here. It sure as hell had a kick to it— arsenic. You don't suppose some of the rats around here are fighting back and slipping arsenic into your whiskey, do you?"

Seth cleared his throat loudly. "Hell, Marshal," he said, "you can't tell nothing about this place." He stepped down

67

the bar toward the lawman. "We got some hardcases in this town who're liable to do anything. But maybe this friend of yours was just sick of living. Could've been suicide, sure enough."

The lawman laughed softly and drank his whiskey. "Don't think so, Bronson. The glass he drank out of was still there in the room, but the bottle was gone. Unless it walked out by itself, the gent who brought the whiskey up to him took the bottle with him when he left."

Seth shrugged. "Well, it ain't no hair off my hide. Barely knew the poor sonofabitch."

"That so, Bronson?"

"There ain't nothing wrong with your hearing, is there?" Seth replied testily, shifting closer. There was an expectant silence growing in the saloon.

The lawman smiled. He was obviously pleased that he had gotten under Seth's skin, and Seth was furious with himself for letting it happen. "The reason I'm surprised at what you just said," the big deputy marshal drawled, "is that it was you—or your brother here—who gave that poor sonofabitch the room without charge."

"He was down and out. He came in here plumb wore out, he did. I just felt it was my duty as a Christian to give him a place to stay for the night. Any law agin that, Marshal?"

"Nope. But there's a law against killing a man. And that's what's been done here." The lawman glanced at the doc. "Would you call it murder, Doctor?"

"The man was obviously poisoned," Beaufort replied easily. "And, as you pointed out, he didn't do it himself."

"Thanks for the drinks," the lawman said, stepping away from the bar.

"Yeah, thanks," said the doctor.

* * *

Seth should have felt better to see the two leave his saloon, but he didn't. He glanced at Luke. His brother was staring at him, his face as white as a sheet. With a quick nod of his head, Seth indicated that Luke should join him at a corner table.

While he waited for Luke to leave the bar, Seth waved over a couple of swampers and told them to get up to room eight and wrap Burt's dead body in a blanket and take it to the undertaker, then clean up the room. As the swampers were leaving, Luke joined Seth at the table and placed two shot glasses and a bottle down between them.

"We got trouble, Seth," Luke said.

"I know that, damn it."

"You heard what Williams said. That man's out for blood. He wasn't working for the government when he sprung Burt. He's off on his own—a law unto himself. And he followed Burt out here for one reason—to get at us."

"And Finn Larson," Seth pointed out.

Luke nodded. "I'm telling you, this Longarm is a tough one. He had Williams scared shitless, and I can see why. He's big enough and tough enough and mean enough. You should hear the tales I've heard about him. How many bullets did Finn say he put in him?"

"That ain't the point. Thing is, how're we gonna get this bastard off our backs? By that I mean, who we goin' to get that's mean enough to do it?"

Luke's eyes lit suddenly. He leaned close. "You thinkin' what I'm thinkin'?"

Seth nodded. "Finn Larson. He sure as hell is mean enough—and he's the bastard got us into this mess in the first place."

69

"But he's gone—lit out! How we goin' to get him back here?"

"I'll send Cal after him. Give him a map. Soon as Finn learns this guy's on his tail, he'll see he has to get back here."

Luke nodded, a glimmer of hope in his eyes. "I sure hope so, Seth. I don't mind telling you, that guy scares me."

"Who do you mean? Finn Larson—or this Longarm?"

"Both of them."

"Me, too. That settles it. I'll go get Cal now."

Upstairs in his room, Longarm wearily unbuckled his gunbelt and hung it over the bedpost. Next, he levered a fresh cartridge into the firing chamber of his Winchester and leaned the rifle against the wall, making sure it was within reach of his pillow. Walking to the window then, he looked out, aware of the constant swell of sound from the saloon below, the clip-clop of horses being ridden into town even at this late hour.

But he would sleep nevertheless, he realized. It had been that kind of day. And he did not think the Warners—who were now calling themselves Jim and Tom Bronson—would move in on him tonight. He had caught the surprise, panic even, in their faces when he'd appeared in the saloon a few minutes ago. With the murder of Burt Williams still heavy on their souls, they would not have the stomach for more slaughter this soon.

But he did not believe that either of those two men had brought that whiskey up to Burt Williams. In that depraved act, Longarm recognized the fine hand of Finn Larson. The Warners had called upon their resident butcher to take care of Williams. And they would call on Finn Larson again. Of that Longarm was certain.

And on that he was counting.

Longarm turned from the window and headed for his bed, undressing quickly. A moment later, despite the racket from the saloon below, he slipped into a deep, sound sleep.

Chapter 5

Finn raised his hand to strike again. But when Ellen cowered back, he reconsidered. Her face was still swollen and discolored from yesterday. He might even have knocked a few of her front teeth loose, and he guessed maybe he didn't want to make her look any worse than she already did. She had been a pretty fair-looking squaw when he first brought her here.

He stepped back away from her and sat down at the table. She straightened warily, letting her hand fall from her face. She was still dry-eyed, still defiant, he noted with grudging respect.

"I don't want no more lip, woman!" he told her. "I'm hungry and I want my breakfast."

Sullenly she went to the cupboard over the sink and pulled down the coffee pot and the can of coffee. Filling the pot from the bucket of well water she had just lugged into the kitchen, she threw in the coffee and slammed the pot down onto the stove. Glancing only once in Finn's direction, she built up the fire with kindling she took from the wood box. As the fire began to thunder in the stove's gut, she brought out the bacon and began slicing generous chunks and slapping them into the frying pan.

Soon the small cabin was filled with the welcome aroma of frying bacon and steaming coffee. Finn leaned back in his chair, satisfied. The woman did have spunk, that was for damn sure. As soon as he had stepped into the cabin the evening before, she had lifted a rifle and aimed it at his gut with a determined look on her face. She wanted him to take her back to Landusky and Ma Ridley's. She wasn't going to spend another day in this prison, she told Finn.

He had pulled up, amused. The rifle she had most likely found in the back room. Striding calmly over to her, he had ripped it from her hands and proceeded to punish her a little, without bothering to tell her, of course, that the rifle could not have been fired—that its firing pin had long since been blown away by a faulty cartridge.

After the beating—to show her there were no hard feelings—he had taken her. She had put up quite a battle as usual, but he was used to that. And in the end, like always, she had submitted and he had taken his measure of her. Yes sir, he thought, chuckling to himself as he recalled it, he sure as hell had done that.

He had brought some presents for her back from Landusky—two dresses, a bonnet, and a shawl. Because of the way she had greeted his return, however, he had not yet given them to her. And he was resolved to hold off a while longer, until she showed him a little more appreciation. He stirred restlessly and realized he was hoping that would be soon. He liked her spunk, all right. There was no denying that. But at the same time he was eager to see the gratitude in her eyes when she opened the packages and saw what he had brought her.

Abruptly, the sound of thundering hooves broke into Finn's thoughts.

Jesus God! he thought. *Who the hell could that be?*

He jumped up from the table and bolted from the cabin, his palms poised above the butts of his sixguns. He could hardly believe his eyes. Young Cal Swinnerton—a tow-headed lickspittle Luke and Seth were making use of around the Silver Slipper—was approaching. And that meant them two sonsofbitches had sent him.

Riding up to the waiting Finn, Cal dismounted hurriedly. He was rubbing the small of his back. "Hell, Finn! My whole backside is raw from following you through these here mountains! How the hell did you find a place so hid away like this?"

"That's my business, Cal. What I want to know is how in blazes *you* found this valley."

"That's easy," the young man said with a grin. "Mr. Bronson gave me a map."

"A map?"

"Yup. But I still had a devil of a time finding this place."

Finn did his best to mask his fury. It was his own damn fault for letting Seth accompany him to this valley the first year after he had found it, he realized. But knowing that did not help at all.

"You got that map, Cal?"

"Right here," Cal said, patting his vest pocket. "But you better hurry on back to Landusky. They sure do want you back there. There's hell breaking loose."

"You want to spell that out, Cal?"

"Here," Cal said, handing Finn a folded piece of paper. "Bronson sent you this note."

Finn took it from Cal, unfolded it, and read:

* * *

*You better get back here, Finn. That feller you
messed with on the Glendale train is already here in
Landusky. There ain't no telling what Burt told him.
So we reckon you got a stake in stopping him before
he gets any closer to that valley of yours. Luke and
I are counting on you. We'll be burying Burt tomorrow.*

Finn crumpled the message. They wanted him back, did
they? They despised him as a killer—but they sure as hell
didn't hesitate to ask him to do their killing for them.

No more.

He had what he wanted here, and he wasn't going to
take any chances on losing it by going back to Landusky
to pull the Warners' chestnuts out of the fire.

Ellen, standing in the cabin doorway behind them, spoke
up. "Step in, Cal, and rest awhile. Breakfast's ready and
there's a fresh pot of coffee on."

At sight of Ellen, Cal whipped off his Stetson. "Thank
you, Miss Ellen. Sure smells good. How you been?"

Ellen sent a swift, hateful glance at Finn, then looked
back at Cal. "Just fine, Cal. It's good to see you again.
How's Ma?"

"She's just fine, Miss Ellen. She brought in some real
swell girls from Kansas City last month."

Ellen smiled, then stepped back to let the two men in.
As Cal passed her in the doorway, Finn stayed where he
was. "Looks like I got business in Landusky," he told Ellen.
"You feed Cal here while I go saddle up my horse."

Finn saw the pure, unadulterated relief pass for an instant
across Ellen's face at this news. Unaccountably it angered
him. He shook it off, however, as he turned and hurried
toward the barn to saddle up his horse.

* * *

Finn had let Cal ride ahead of him and had noted how skillfully the young rider had been able to find his way back to the stream. This convinced him that his decision to kill Cal was the right one.

He waited until they were both high on the ridge trail before he made his move. Spurring his mount gently, Finn drew closer to Cal. "Better let me lead the way."

Cal pulled back on his reins, expecting Finn to ride past him on the outside. Instead, Finn pulled alongside Cal on the inside of the trail. He saw the startled look on Cal's face as Finn's horse nudged his own closer to the cliff's edge.

Once alongside Cal, Finn pulled up and patted the neck of his horse to settle it down. His mount was shaking its head unhappily. When he had calmed the horse, he looked at Cal.

"You got that map Bronson gave you?"

Cal nodded nervously. He was having some difficulty keeping his mount from spooking. "It's in my pocket," he answered.

"I want it."

"Now?"

"Now!"

"Jesus, Finn, can't it wait till we get off this trail?"

"I said now, Cal."

"Damn you, Finn!" Cal muttered, reaching into his vest pocket.

As soon as Finn's fingers closed about the map, he drew his right sixgun and swung it viciously. The gun barrel thudded heavily as it crunched through the crown of Cal's Stetson and struck the young man's skull. Screaming in pain and anger, Cal tried to ward off Finn's second blow with an upraised forearm.

But Finn struck again and again, surprised at Cal's ability to remain in the saddle. At last, one furious blow shattered

Cal's forearm, sounding like the crack of a dry log in a fireplace. Yet still Cal hung on, his head down, his good arm holding desperately onto Finn. But he was weakening now. One final, vicious blow to his head did it, and Cal toppled from his mount.

He almost took his horse over the edge with him, but the terrified animal yanked its head back and planted its four feet firmly. Cal lost the reins. Scrambling frantically for a handhold with his one good hand, he disappeared over the lip of the ridge. His cry carried far before it ended abruptly among the rocks well below the trail.

Finn dismounted and looked over, still panting from the fierce exertion. He could see Cal's body wedged into a narrow cleft far below. Cal was dead for sure. Finn glanced up at the sky. There were no buzzards yet. But soon they would notice Cal's still body and pick him clean.

Turning, Finn slapped the rump of Cal's mount and sent it on down the trail. If the horse found its way back to Landusky, it might tell the Warners what they had not yet come to realize—that Finn Larson had meant it when he vowed that he was through with them for good. He had taken care of Burt Williams for them. Now it was their turn. Longarm was their problem.

Finn swung into his saddle and slowly, cautiously turned his horse around, anxious to get back to the cabin. He was still hungry for that breakfast Ellen had started.

And he was hungry for her as well.

Longarm and Beaufort were leaving Bim's restaurant the following day just before sundown when they saw a riderless horse trotting past them. The sight of the gelding caused someone in front of the Silver Slipper to cry out, and at once the small knot of loafers lounging on the saloon's porch left it to follow the horse. As these men knew only

78

too well, a riderless horse always meant trouble.

Longarm and the doc followed after them.

The hostler—his name was Gabe Parnell, Longarm had learned—appeared in the large open doorway of the livery. At sight of the approaching horse, he hurried out to meet it. At once he noted the way the horse favored its right front foot.

"Who took this horse out, Gabe?" Longarm asked, pushing his way through the small crowd.

As he let the gelding satisfy its thirst at the street trough, Gabe glanced up at Longarm. "Cal Swinnerton."

"Cal?" someone cried. "You sure, Gabe?"

"You heard me, damn it!"

At once the fellow turned and hurried back toward the saloon.

Gabe led the horse into the livery, Longarm and the doc following close behind. "Who is this Cal Swinnerton, Gabe?" Longarm asked.

His attention still focused on the horse's pronounced limp, Gabe said, "Cal hangs around the Silver Slipper." He glanced up at Longarm. "He had a map Bronson gave him when he left. Had to find someone who was hid pretty good, looked like." Gabe turned and led the gelding carefully into a stall. "I wonder if he found him."

Longarm turned about to face Beaufort. "Do you know Cal?"

"Not to speak to," Beaufort replied. "But he's one of Ma's steady customers. A towhead with blue eyes. A nice kid, maybe not overly bright, but eager to please. The Bronsons have been making good use of him lately."

Gabe had finished unsaddling the horse by this time. As Longarm watched, the hostler lifted the gelding's right foreleg. "Split a hoof back there somewheres after throwing a shoe," Gabe announced. "Musta sure been rough country.

Lucky he made it back." Gabe let the horse's leg down gently, then patted the animal affectionately on the neck.

At that moment Jim Bronson—or the man calling himself Jim Bronson—burst into the livery. The fellow who had bolted back to the saloon to get him was close on his heels.

"What's all this, Gabe?" Bronson demanded. "Where's Cal Swinnerton?"

Gabe shrugged wearily. "Beats the shit out of me, Mr. Bronson," he said. "But this here horse is as gentle as a kitten. If he throwed Cal, it must've been a rattler or something that spooked him."

Jim Bronson swung around to face the growing crowd. "Any volunteers?" he bellowed. "We need to send out a search party to find Cal. He might be lying somewhere with his ribs all stove in! We'll need ten men at least, and we'll be out for some time, looks like."

Not a single man stepped forward. Instead, with heads averted, the men in the crowd turned about and slunk off down the street. From their ranks came a few barks of cynical laughter. They had no stomach for hard riding. Not for Cal Swinnerton. Not for anyone, Longarm realized. This town was filled with no-accounts, hardcases with only one concern—their own appetites.

Bronson turned back to glare at Longarm and the doc. For a moment it appeared he might ask them to join his search party. But only for a moment. Swallowing his frustration, the man stalked back out of the livery and strode swiftly up the street to his saloon.

Watching him go, Gabe began to brush down the animal. "Got me a bar-shoe," he said. "Should fix this here animal's hoof in no time. But there ain't nothing I know of can fix that feller's misery. He sent Cal on an errand, and now Cal ain't a-comin' back from it."

"Who do you think he sent Cal after, Gabe?" asked the doc.

Longarm took out a cheroot and handed it to the hostler. He thumbed a sulfur match to life and held it to the tip of the cheroot until the hostler got it going.

Gabe sucked the smoke greedily into his lungs. "I think he sent Cal after that feller you was lookin' for, Marshal. The one you described to me. That feller who rode out with two pack horses the night you rode into town."

"Finn Larson."

"That's right. He's been mighty thick with them two since they bought the Silver Slipper. I figure he knows them from somewhere. But Finn's a mean one, so I never let myself get too curious about him. One thing I know for sure, though. He damn well never intends to let anyone know where it is he holes up."

The doc looked at Longarm. "I understand Finn's used this town for years," he said. "From what I gather, Ma Ridley and her girls are pretty well terrified of the man. He's got a murderous reputation."

Gabe took the cheroot out of his mouth and spat. "He's a cold-blooded killer. There ain't a man in this town'd tangle with him."

"Quite so," agreed the doctor. He looked back at Longarm. "Last time Finn visited Ma's place, she bought him off with one of her girls."

"Maybe you better explain that to me, Doc."

"The girl in question was certain she could handle Finn. She put up quite a battle, in fact. But it seemed that only whetted Finn's appetite. He liked her so much, he offered to buy her from Ma. Ma said no, but Finn got nasty. Very nasty. The girl saw what trouble she was causing and went with Finn—for a price."

"How much?"

"Three hundred dollars, I believe. Ma's keeping it for her. I suppose the girl had some crazy idea she could get away from Finn whenever she took a mind to—but she's been gone for close to a year."

"She still with him, do you think?"

Beaufort nodded. "I'd say so. Word is, last time he was in town, he bought some dresses."

Longarm looked back at Gabe. "You said Cal had a map. Any idea what section of this country was on that map?"

Gabe nodded. "Cal had some trouble reading it. I saw him squint at it a couple of times and then mutter to me about a hell of a long ride into the mountains past Deer River country."

"And when did he leave, exactly?"

"Not long after you found that dead man in the hotel."

"He left that same night?"

"Yes sir, Marshal. He sure did."

Longarm nodded grimly. He had guessed right. They had sent for Finn Larson, as he had known they would. Only Finn Larson, it appeared, had decided he was not going to join this particular party.

"Thanks, Gabe," Longarm told the hostler, starting from the stable with Beaufort.

A moment later, as the two men were crossing the street to the hotel, the doc said, "You want to tell me what this is all about, Marshal?"

"I think maybe it's time I did, at that," Longarm acknowledged, "since I'm going to be needing your help soon enough, I'm thinking. Let's find a quiet spot on the hotel porch."

About half an hour later, as had been his custom since arriving in Landusky, Longarm entered his room cautiously, closed the door and locked it, and began packing his small

82

store of necessities. That task completed, he took out his double-action Colt .44-40.

Swinging the gun over the bed, he emptied the cylinder on the sheets and dry-fired a few times to test the action. Then, using a small, oily cloth he carried in one of his saddlebags, he wiped the gun thoroughly, after which he inspected the firing pin to make sure it was not fouled. Then he reloaded the revolver with fresh cartridges, holding each cartridge up to the light of the lamp before thumbing it home. Usually, as a safety precaution, he carried only five rounds in the six chambers, with the hammer resting on the empty chamber, but this time he filled each chamber. Replacing the .44 in the holster of his cross-draw rig, he proceeded to check out the derringer with the same meticulous care.

Satisfied at last, he took up his Winchester and bedroll, slung his saddlebags over his shoulder, and left the room on his way to the livery stable. He was pretty damn sure that, if he lived, he would not be at all welcome in Landusky before this night passed.

Stepping through the Silver Slipper's batwings a few moments later, Longarm was greeted with a silence almost as total as it was sudden. Every face in the saloon turned instantly in his direction. But only for a moment—then most of the men looked quickly, furtively, away. This was the first time he had entered the saloon since the night Burt Williams had been murdered; but Longarm recognized many of the same unshaven, grimy hardcases he had seen in the place that night.

Only the saloon girls—many of them too old for their roles as seductive enticers and looking somewhat pathetic in their faded red-spangled skirts and low-cut blouses— seemed not in the least intimidated by Longarm's sudden appearance. As Longarm walked deliberately across the saloon floor toward the poker games in the rear, the girls appraised him with frank, challenging stares, then turned their attention back to the patrons they were working. But their voices seemed unnaturally loud and out of place. At last they, too, fell silent.

By the time Longarm reached the corner table where Seth Warner was playing poker, the saloon had grown so quiet that the chink of his spurs punctuated each step he took with unnatural clarity.

"Mind if I sit in?" Longarm asked Seth.

"We already got enough players at this table, Marshal," Warner replied, his face ashen. "There's other tables and other players glad to take your money."

Doc Beaufort was sitting at Warner's table, his back to Longarm. He coughed slightly, then scraped his chair back. "You may take my place, Marshal," he said. "My luck has been positively abominable."

"Thanks, Doc," Longarm said, sitting down in the chair. "I've been waiting to play in this here game since first I rode into Landusky. You might say I came a long way to play with my good friend Seth Warner."

"Name's Bronson," Seth snapped, furious. "You'd best remember that."

"Bullshit, Warner. Since you're the oldest one, you'd be Seth Warner. And that brother of yours behind the bar would be Luke. But, hell, you don't have to admit who you are if you don't want to. This here saloon probably has more aliases at this moment than the entire Warner gang ever had. Now, what do you say we play cards?"

Longarm turned to Luke Warner standing behind the bar. "Let's have some chips, Luke," he called, slapping silver coins down onto the table. "We'll start with a hundred. Give this here pot some spice right off."

As Luke, his face dark with suppressed fury, brought the

chips, Longarm asked for a fresh deck. When it was slapped grudgingly down before him, he opened the deck, cut it, and passed it across to Seth Warner.

The game began.

It was much later, and Longarm was winning. The pile of chips in front of him was considerably higher than the meager pile sitting before Seth Warner. The saloon's other games had folded soon after this one began and the bar was clean of drinkers as everyone in the place, including Luke Warner, crowded around the table to watch.

The other two players at the table with Longarm and Seth—caught up in the game like sand in a dust devil—had remained in the game, contributing little more than occasional bets and a few barely audible remarks. The game was really just between Longarm and Seth Warner. And everyone in the saloon knew it.

Longarm was dealing swiftly and expertly, the sound of the cards slicking over the table clearly audible in the big room. Abruptly, a card Longarm dealt himself skidded to the floor. Though Longarm snatched up the exposed card in a twinkling and had kept the deck out of sight of the other players for only an instant, Seth was quick to call it.

"Misdeal!" he cried. "New deck!"

"Since when?" Longarm demanded. "It was my card. I keep it. There's no need for a new deck."

"House rule, damn your eyes!" snarled Seth. "Ain't that right?" he asked his brother.

Luke Warner nodded quickly. "Sure. That's right. A house rule."

Longarm shrugged, pushed the already dealt cards to one side, and leaned back as a new deck was brought and the game continued.

Two hands later, Longarm, having just discarded two

cards, drew a pair of kings. He had drawn to three aces. A glance across the table showed him that Seth Warner was pleased with his hand.

"Table stakes, Warner?" Longarm asked.

He had been goading Seth all during the game by addressing him as Warner instead of his assumed name—until at last the fellow had begun to answer to it, a dogged defiance burning in his eyes as he thus admitted his true identity to Longarm and those crowding about the table.

Eyes lighting craftily, Warner nodded. "Sure. Table stakes."

"How much you got in front of you?"

Warner counted his chips swiftly. "One hundred and twenty."

Longarm had already counted his winnings. The pot contained better than fifty dollars. "I've got one hundred and sixty," Longarm told Warner. "And I'm betting it all. You planning on matching it?"

Warner looked quickly over at his brother. Luke nodded bleakly.

"The house will cover your bet," Seth said, pushing into the pot what chips remained in front of him. "And I'm calling you."

Longarm pushed his own chips into the pot, then fanned his cards and set them down faceup. There was a startled murmur when the crowd saw Longarm's full house, ace high. With a furious cry Seth flung down his own hand— two pairs, jacks and queens.

Longarm chuckled and reached out for the chips. But as he did so, two playing cards—both of them aces—slipped out of his shirt cuff and landed faceup on the table.

Warner's face went livid. From the start, Longarm had been crowding him, doing his best to make the man react violently. Longarm's intentions were clear—and far more final than winning at poker. Aware of this, Seth had hung grimly on to his composure, obviously determined to do nothing that would give Longarm an excuse to draw on him.

Now, however, the sight of those two aces swept away his resolve—as Longarm had known it would.

"You've been cheatin' me!" Warner cried, clawing for his sixgun.

But as Warner jumped to his feet, Longarm drove the table sharply at him. Its edge caught Warner's gun hand. Continuing to ram the table ruthlessly forward, Longarm slammed Warner back against the wall and drew his own .44.

Everyone scrambled back out of the line of fire as Luke bolted for the bar. Still pinning Warner to the wall, Longarm heard Doc Beaufort's warning cry. Longarm spun around to see Luke Warner, behind the bar by this time, hauling a shotgun into view. Crabbing swiftly to one side, Longarm fired at Luke.

The round slammed into the mirror behind Luke, webbing the glass. Luke ducked swiftly out of sight. Longarm spun back to face Seth and found him out from behind the table, both hands about his gun as he steadied his aim. Longarm flung up his gun and fired.

The bullet struck Seth just above the heart, stamping a dark hole in his blue vest. The force of the slug slammed Seth back against the wall. His back braced solidly against it, he managed to get off a shot at Longarm. The round ticked Longarm's hat brim. Longarm brought up his gun and fired a second time, blowing a hole in Seth's gut. Gasping, Seth dropped his sixgun, then sagged slowly to his knees.

Another warning shout came from Beaufort. As Longarm spun back to face the bar, he saw Beaufort fire at Luke Warner. The round struck Luke in the face, opening a hole just below his right cheekbone. The hole appeared to swallow the bottom of Luke's entire face. Dropping the shotgun, Luke grabbed at his disintegrating face with both hands, then sank out of sight behind the bar.

Longarm turned to face the saloon's sullen patrons. Several were standing with their hands resting lightly on the butts of their sixguns, but not one of them seemed anxious to make a play. A tall fellow with a black patch over his right eye pushed his way through the crowd and held up. Longarm had heard this fellow referred to as Blacky.

"You got 'em both, Long," Blacky drawled. "And you made your point, sure enough. They were the Warners, just like you said—the same two who robbed the Glendale train. I heard you was there and got shot up pretty bad. But you didn't have no legal warrant for what you just done." Blacky smiled. "So we figure that puts you on the same level with the rest of us here."

He glanced at Doc Beaufort.

"That goes for you, too, Doc."

"I'm flattered," the doctor replied, dropping his smoking Colt into the black leather holster at his hip.

Blacky looked back at Longarm. "You got enemies here, Marshal. But there ain't none of us don't respect you. From what I hear, you was always fair with them you tracked. We'll be the same." Blacky took out a large gold watch and consulted it. "It ain't midnight yet. We'll give you both an hour to get out of town. Then we'll come after you."

"Fair enough," said Longarm. He glanced at Beaufort. "Sorry I got you into this, Doc."

"Forget it," said Beaufort. "I'll be glad to shake the dust of this town."

"Then let's go."

A few minutes later, Longarm galloped out of Landusky astride his black, the doc riding at his side. He was not surprised when a shot exploded in the darkness behind them. Not all of Landusky's gunslicks were as willing as Blacky to give Longarm that fair running start he'd promised.

Chapter 6

High into the Absarokas the two men rode, Blacky and his gang of gunslicks pursuing them with surprising tenacity. Only once during the night did Longarm and Beaufort make camp, relying on the cloak of darkness to ensure their safety. It was near dawn when the thunder of hoofs and the shouts of their pursuers echoing in the canyons behind them sent them once more on their way.

At dawn they broke out of the mountains and galloped into the Deer River valley. Passing a stand of small pines huddled along the banks of a mountain stream, Longarm noticed that this was the only cover on the valley floor. A glance around him showed an almost continuous wall of rock hemming them in. He considered for a moment, then made up his mind.

"That way," he called to the doc, pointing to a steep slope beyond the pines.

After a long, steady gallop, they reached the foot of the slope and started their horses up the steep grade. The footing was difficult, but they urged their horses on and kept going until an outcropping of rock stopped them. Dismounting, Longarm coaxed his black around the obstacle and found a passable but quite steep trail, enabling them to continue on up the slope.

They were forced to dismount and lead their horses up the remaining hundred or so yards to the rim of the canyon. By the time they had pulled their skittish mounts up onto the rim after them, Doc Beaufort was coughing steadily. Before Longarm could reach him, the man toppled to the ground, his handkerchief held up to his mouth. Through eyes narrowed in pain, Beaufort peered unhappily up at Longarm. "Leave me behind, Longarm," the man gasped. "I'll stop the bastards."

"We'll stop them together. I'm not leaving you behind."

"What's your plan?"

"We'll pin them in those pines until dark. Then we'll go down and get them. You game?"

Beaufort nodded, his handkerchief once more held up to his mouth as a second paroxysm of coughing seized him.

Not long after, Blacky and four riders appeared below them on the valley floor. They were heading directly for the pines. Longarm had no difficulty making out Blacky—or rather, the dark patch over his right eye.

Following Longarm's and the doc's tracks, Blacky veered away from the pines and led his men straight for the ridge where Longarm, his Winchester at the ready, waited. Blacky's riders were strung out behind him, and for Longarm's purposes it would be better if they were more closely bunched.

Abruptly, less than fifty yards from the base of the cliff, Blacky halted his mount and pointed up at the ridge. The riders following were soon bunched about him. It was obvious to Longarm why Blacky had stopped. The man realized that Longarm was probably waiting on the ridge above them at that very moment.

And he was correct.

Longarm turned and nodded to the doc, who was about twenty yards farther along the ridge. Then, sighting carefully, Longarm fired at Blacky. The round came close, but not close enough. It tore off Blacky's hat, causing him to yank his horse about. A moment later he was leading his men on a frantic charge back to the pines as Longarm and the doc added urgency to their flight with a steady fusillade.

Only one rider was unlucky enough to catch a round. He peeled back off his horse and landed heavily on his back. After a moment the man staggered to his feet and limped after his comrades. But he did not go far before he collapsed facedown. This time he did not get up. Longarm signaled to Beaufort to cease fire.

"Now all we got to do is keep the rest of them in those pines," Longarm called over to the doctor.

Beaufort nodded.

For the rest of that long day it was cat and mouse—or two cats and four mice. Every time Blacky and his riders made an effort to break out of the pines, Longarm and the Doc drove them back with a punishing fusillade. Toward the end of the day, when the dusk made visibility at that distance difficult, one rider managed to go some distance before they shot his horse out from under him and sent him scurrying frantically back to cover.

As soon as it was completely dark and before the moon came up, Longarm and Beaufort made their way back down the slope and headed for the pines. It was now two men against four. Not very good odds, but Longarm was counting on surprise and the darkness to even the score. Whatever the odds, he had no intention of allowing Blacky and his gunslicks to dog his trail any further. He could not afford it.

Besides, he did not like Blacky.

They were almost to the pines when Longarm found that Blacky had the same idea. Pushing the doc to the ground beside him, Longarm went flat, his Winchester slamming onto the turf ahead of him. Blacky and the three gunslicks were approaching from the direction of the pines. They were running softly, heads down, sidearms gleaming dully in the dim light filtering down from the starlit sky.

Motioning to the doc to move off to his right, Longarm rolled swiftly in the other direction to give the four men a clear path through them to the ridge. Holding his breath, his rifle trained on Blacky, Longarm watched as the gunmen, looking neither to the right nor to the left, moved swiftly on past them on their way to the ridge.

As soon as they had passed him, Longarm stood up. Beaufort got to his feet also. Longarm levered a fresh cartridge into the firing chamber of his Winchester. In the stillness, the sound of it was like the crack of doom. Blacky and his cohorts spun around. Without waiting for Longarm to fire, they opened up, their sixguns filling the night with lead. As their rounds hummed past him like angry hornets, Longarm went down on one knee and, levering swiftly, began a rapid fire that cut a murderous swath through the four gunmen.

It was over in less than a minute. Cautiously, Longarm stood up, waited a moment longer, then walked toward the downed men, Beaufort joining him. The first man they came to was writhing painfully on the ground, groaning deeply. Longarm put his rifle down and examined him as best he could in the darkness. There was a bloody patch on his right side. Though the man appeared to be in considerable pain, it did not look as if he had sustained a serious wound.

Beaufort and Longarm left him and inspected the next two gunmen sprawled in the grass. They were both dead. Blacky was lying on his side. His legs were drawn up under him, his back a dark, gleaming mess in the darkness. Beaufort knelt by the man to examine his wound.

With a deep, guttural curse, Blacky rolled over onto his back, flung up his sixgun, and fired into Beaufort. As Beaufort staggered back, Longarm emptied his .44 into Blacky. He was so intent on finishing Blacky that he did not hear the first gunman they had examined closing in on him from behind until it was almost too late.

Longarm spun around, bringing up his left arm to protect himself. The fellow struck down at him with the barrel of his sixgun. The blow almost broke the lawman's forearm as it drove him down onto one knee. Enraged, his wounded assailant kicked Longarm in the face. The blow knocked Longarm backward into the grass. His .44 was empty, and Longarm flung it at the gunslick. The fellow ducked easily, then, chuckling coldly, carefully aimed his revolver at Longarm.

"You sonofabitch, Longarm," the fellow breathed. "You don't remember me. Maybe you don't remember my brother neither. You brought him in four years ago. Tim Watts. He's rottin' in Yuma now. This is for him, you miserable bastard."

But before he could pull the trigger, Longarm clawed his derringer out of his vest pocket and rolled swiftly to one side. Watts fired at Longarm's rolling form and missed. He didn't get a second chance as Longarm crabbed swiftly to his left and fired both of the derringer's barrels at the gunman. Each round caught the man in his chest. Watts staggered back, then sank to his knees. He managed to cock his revolver one more time, but discharged the bullet into the ground as he toppled forward lifeless.

Scrambling to his feet, Longarm hurried to Beaufort's side. The man was conscious.

"Where are you hit, Doc?"

"He caught me in the right side, just under my ribs," Beaufort managed to gasp. "Feels like it tore a mean hole on its way through. I just might live if I can get somewhere to clean out the wound and stop the bleeding."

"I'll get the horses. Are there any settlements near here? Any farms or ranches?"

"The other side of this valley," Beaufort gasped, his voice rasping painfully. "Northwest . . . way we were headed when we broke for the ridge."

He began to cough then, but he was too weak to hold his handkerchief up to his mouth. As Longarm watched, the man's eyes closed and his head sank back onto the grass. Only then did his painful, tearing cough cease.

As Longarm pulled up, the settler stepped out of his rude log cabin, a shotgun cradled in his arms. Behind him came a tow-headed boy of seven or eight, and behind him an astonishingly beautiful woman in her early twenties—obviously the young boy's sister. Her cheekbones stood out almost gauntly, but her dark amber eyes mirrored a glowing, robust health.

"You from Landusky, mister?" the settler asked. "If so, you ain't welcome."

Longarm ignored the man, dismounted, and pulled the doc gently out of his saddle. Beaufort was barely conscious, but he managed a weak smile, nevertheless, as Longarm swung the doc into his arms and proceeded to carry him into the sodbuster's cabin. At first the settler seemed inclined to bar his way, but when the tall red-headed woman stepped

96

quickly back to let him enter, the man lost his hostility and followed meekly in after him.

"Put him down on that cot in the corner," the red-headed woman instructed.

Longarm did as she suggested. Then he stepped back. The young woman leaned close over the doc, took one look at his blood-soaked frock coat, and pulled it off. A moment later she took off his shirt as well, gasping slightly when she saw the wound under Beaufort's right ribcage.

Beaufort opened his eyes and smiled up at the woman. "I'm a doctor, ma'am," he told her quietly. "If you'll be kind enough to follow my instructions, I foresee no difficulty at all in cleaning up this mess."

"Of course," the girl said, glancing with some surprise at Longarm.

At that moment Longarm heard the sound of others entering the cabin. He spun about and found himself face to face once again with Bill Miller and his daughter Laura. Miller had a Winchester at the ready and seemed primed to use it until he recognized Longarm. With a sudden, relieved smile, he lowered the rifle.

"Why, Mr. Long!" Laura cried. "What are you doing here?"

Indicating his wounded companion with a glance, Longarm explained their need for shelter. At once Miller and his daughter introduced Longarm to the settler. His name was Ron Walker; his daughter was Cynthia, and the boy was called Billy.

These were the relatives who were helping Miller and his daughter settle in the area. Since the Walkers had not been welcomed wholeheartedly by the cattlemen in the area, cowpokes on their way to and from Landusky had taken to deviling Walker's place—and especially his pretty daughter. This was the reason for his cool reception of Longarm.

97

When Billy had warned his father of Longarm's approach, Walker had suggested to Miller that he arm himself and hide with Laura in a gully within sight of the cabin.

Once the introductions were completed, Beaufort's condition brought both girls swiftly to his side. With gentle skill, they followed the physician's remarkably calm instructions as he directed the cleaning out and flushing of his wound. Hot soap and water combined with raw whiskey was what the doctor told them to use. As the two women labored over the jagged hole in his side—at one point cutting away the dead flesh with red-hot shears—the pain was so great that Beaufort momentarily passed out. But, for the most part, he remained conscious, only lowering his voice on occasion when the pain became too intense. At no time was he short with the women. His patience throughout was remarkable.

As soon as the wound was clean, Beaufort directed Laura in the bandaging that succeeded finally in stemming the flow of blood. Unfortunately, there was nothing the physician could do to put color back into his gaunt cheeks or to prevent the racking cough that began to tear at his lungs once the operation was complete.

By nightfall, Laura managed to get a bowl of hot broth down Beaufort's throat. This seemed to quiet the man noticeably and he was soon asleep. Laura insisted on remaining on a chair beside the cot, however, her eyes on the physician. It was obvious that Beaufort's courage had impressed her mightily.

As Longarm opened his bedroll under the stars that night, he was visited by Cynthia and Billy. He had selected a wooded knoll within sight of the cabin, and as Cynthia came up to him in the darkness, she seemed pleased.

98

"This is my favorite spot," she told him. "I come here whenever I get to feeling down."

"Me, too," piped up Billy. "There's a water hole on the far side of this timber. It's almost dried up now."

Longarm smiled. "That's too bad," he said to Billy.

"If you want, Mr. Long," Billy said eagerly, "I could bring my straw mattress out here and keep you company. I like to camp out."

"That's all right, Billy," Longarm told the boy. "I like to camp out myself. There are times when I prefer it." He glanced at Cynthia. "That cabin of yours is mighty crowded by now. You tell your Pa I don't mind sleeping out here at all. How's the doc?"

Cynthia smiled. In the darkness, her eyes and teeth seemed to glow. She was a very lovely young woman. "He's still sleeping. And Laura is still at his side. I think she likes Beaufort."

"He's not a man one is likely to forget. He saved my life in Landusky—and now he's just finished saving his own, at least for now."

She nodded somberly. "He is a very sick man, isn't he? Consumption is a terrible disease. That's what took my aunt and my mother." She looked quickly around her. "But out here the air is so clean, so fresh. Surely the doctor can escape the vapours in this high country."

"I imagine that's why he came West. Or one of the reasons, anyway."

Billy heard something in the trees and ran off to investigate. A moment later he returned. He had seen an owl carrying off a field mouse, he told them, his voice hushed.

"It's time for you to get back to the cabin," Cynthia said to him. "Pa asked me to speak to Mr. Long private."

"Aw, gee, Sis!"

She reached over and ruffled his hair fondly. "Be a good boy, Billy. We got a lot to do tomorrow. More logs to cut for Uncle Bill's cabin. And we'll need your help for that. You'll be driving the team again."

The boy brightened. He turned to Longarm. "Goodnight, Mr. Long," he said. "Watch out for Indians!"

They watched him race off across the dark meadow toward the cabin. When he had vanished into the night, Cynthia sat down in the grass beside Longarm. "If you came from Landusky, Mr. Long, perhaps you can help us."

"Of course, if I can. What is it?"

"Laura told me about you, Mr. Long," she said softly, a trace of a smile on her face. "She also told me that you know about her sister, Ellen."

"Yes, I do."

"Did you see her in Landusky, Mr. Long?"

"No. If she resembles Laura, I would have recognized her if I had."

Cynthia frowned. "That's too bad. I was hoping that . . . since you and the doctor were such good friends . . ."

"What has that got to do with it?"

"We all know, Mr. Long, where Doctor Beaufort spends most of his time in Landusky."

"At Ma Ridley's."

"Yes."

Longarm frowned. "And you think I might have met Laura's sister at Ma's."

"If not you, then perhaps Doctor Beaufort has."

"In other words, Ellen was one of Ma Ridley's girls."

"I'm afraid that's true, Mr. Long. My father intended to visit Ma's place and tell Ellen that her father was on the way here. He was hoping this would give Ellen the courage to leave Ma. She could move in with us and nothing further would need to be said about her...former employment."

"And?"

"When my father did visit Ma's, she told him that Ellen was no longer with her, that she had found other employment."

"Other employment? In Landusky?"

Cynthia nodded. "But my father looked everywhere for her, and after a while he became certain that quite a few people knew where she was, but were afraid to tell him. So at last he gave up."

"I see. Well, I assure you, Cynthia, I did not see Ellen while I was in Landusky. If she resembles her sister as much as Laura says she does, seems like I would have recalled seeing her."

"I suppose that's true." Cynthia sighed. "Anyway, I tried. Pa thought there just might be the chance. Tomorrow, first chance I get, I'll ask the doctor." She leaned her head wearily back against a tree trunk and closed her eyes. "It's so peaceful here. You should sleep well tonight."

"I hope so. I could use the sleep."

Cynthia began to stretch, uttering a tiny cry of delight as she arched her long body. Finished, she pulled her knees up to her breasts and hugged her legs. "You know, Mr. Long," she said, her emerald eyes glowing as she turned to look deeply into Longarm's, "I'm not the least bit sleepy. I feel like a cat ready to prowl." Then she laughed softly, her voice deep and husky. "Do you think I'm awful for saying that?"

"No. Of course not." Longarm was surprised at the sudden dryness in his throat.

Her nearness was affecting him, despite his own fatigue. He had caught at once the obvious implication of her words. If she was restless, so was he, for that matter. There was

101

as much raw hunger in him at that moment as there was in the woman beside him. He could sense her explosive, pent-up need. He shared it.

"I guess I'd better get back now," Cynthia said, her voice suddenly small.

He was sure he detected a tentative, desperate hope in her voice. He knew without any more prompting what she wanted him to say.

"Don't go, Cynthia. Not right now."

She looked at him searchingly, hopefully. "You . . . want me to stay?"

"If you want to stay."

She said nothing for a moment. Then she released her legs and leaned back against the tree. Staring up at the sky, she said, "You know, don't you? I mean . . . what I need— what any woman out here so long without a man needs. You men have your Ma Ridley's to go to—but all we have is . . ." She bit her lip and stopped.

Longarm said nothing. Instead, he reached out and took one of her hands in his. It was almost feverish.

"Laura told me about you," Cynthia said at last. "She said you were kind and gentle—that you understood about a woman."

He released her hand, then reached up and took her by the shoulders and pulled her over so that she was cradled in his arms. Then he bent gently and kissed her on the lips. She kept her lips immobile. He could feel her trembling— whether with passion or fear, he could not tell for sure. It was quite possible, he knew, that even though every nerve in her body needed to express the desire dammed up within her, she still might jump up and bolt headlong for the cabin. There was, after all, such a thing as wanting something too much.

He kissed her softly on her eyelids and felt her trembling

102

subside somewhat. Then he kissed her behind her ear and blew softly upon her earlobe. Uttering a barely audible cry, she reached her arms up and circled his neck. He bent again to her lips and this time they opened to his gentle probing. Gently biting her lower lip, he began to suck on it. A shuddering sigh came from deep within her, and her mouth began to work with sudden passion as her arms tightened frantically about his neck.

He flipped aside the flap of his soogan and swept her in beside him. After an agony of fumbling, their bodies—completely, feverishly naked—were pressed against each other. He rolled over and mounted her, his lips still clinging to hers.

He bent to her breasts and kissed them, his lips teasing and caressing her nipples until they became erect. She began to moan softly. He moved his lips down her tummy. She gasped in delight. A moment later, lifting his face from her moist curls, he moved swiftly up over her like a great cat and mounted her, thrusting firmly without constraint, aware only of her need and his...

Later, much later, when they had drunk their fill of each other, Cynthia clung to him, her head pressed against his chest.

"That was worth waiting for, Mr. Long," she said in a small, contented voice. "Laura was right. You do know how to pleasure a woman. I hope my response was satisfactory, as well."

He chuckled and kissed her gently. "It was," he told her truthfully. "And my friends call me Longarm," he reminded her. "From now on I would be happy to regard you as one."

Cynthia laughed, and for a moment they lay in each other's arms, content.

At last he stirred. "You'd better get back," he said reluctantly. "Your father will wonder."

103

"Yes," she admitted with a sigh, "he will."

She leaned away from him and flung back the soogan's flap and stood up. There was enough light from the stars to give him a clear view of her. Awed by her flawless beauty, he lay on his back, staring up at her. She smiled down at him for a moment and did not move, allowing him to feast his eyes; then she reached down for her things and began to dress.

A moment later, a dim, spectral figure moving through the moonless night, she paused on her way back to the cabin and waved good night to him.

The next morning, Ron Walker insisted on extending his hospitality to Beaufort until the physician was well enough to ride again. Propped up by three down pillows, Beaufort smiled wanly and did not protest. Beside him, Laura beamed and did what she could to plump up Beaufort's pillows so that he would be more comfortable.

"Looks like you'll be in good hands, Doc," Longarm said, smiling at Laura. The girl blushed.

Longarm shook the doctor's hand and left the cabin with Ron Walker and Cynthia as Bill Miller, having completed harnessing the wagon for the day's log hauling, joined them. Before mounting up, Longarm asked them for descriptions of any cowpokes or other riders they might have glimpsed passing through the valley during the past week.

"Any particular rider?" Walker asked.

Longarm described Finn Larson.

Cynthia spoke up. "I might have seen such a man, but I can't be sure. There was a rider with two pack horses on the horizon for a while less than a week back."

"Which way was he going?"

"Toward those peaks in the distance."

"The Deer River range," Walker said.

"Thanks," Longarm said, mounting up. "Looks like that's where I'm heading then."

He thanked Ron Walker for his hospitality and nodded goodbye to Cynthia. Then, touching the brim of his Stetson to Billy, who was watching from the cabin doorway, he set off in the direction of the Deer River range.

"Be careful, Longarm!" Cynthia called.

Longarm waved, then turned back around in his saddle. He knew he could not be sure that the rider Cynthia had glimpsed was indeed Finn Larson, but right now it was the only lead he had. The two weeks he had requested from Billy Vail had long since been spent, and as far as Longarm knew, he was no longer a deputy U.S. marshal. But that really did not matter to him.

All he wanted now was to get his hands on that butcher, Finn Larson.

Chapter 7

The Deer River Range was a younger one than the Absarokas with even more spectacular peaks, fewer trees and
less grassland. It was cut by a lacework of swift mountain
streams fed by the two snow-capped peaks which dominated
the range, Horsehead Peak and Bridger Peak.

By mid-afternoon Longarm had left the foothills and was
well inside the range, keeping to a narrow game trail that
followed alongside the Deer River, at this point in its
young career a lusty, swift-moving mountain stream. On
both sides of the stream, sheer cliff walls loomed almost
straight up. Masses of white rock leaned out from the sides
of the rock faces, resembling great cauliflowers of stone
that had congealed on the canyons' massive flanks. Occasional stands of pine, their roots fixed into the sides of the
cliff like giant claws, somehow managed to grow upon a
few narrow ledges.

For the most part, however, the landsacpe was barren
of trees and grass. Only rock—sheer, precipitous, as gaunt
as the ribs of oxen bleaching in the sun—belonged here.

Riding through this vaulting landscape, Longarm could not help but feel dwarfed, intimidated even.

He had ridden no more than a few miles into the range when he became aware of two vultures lifting into the sky over his head. They were drifting heavily, sluggishly, toward the lip of a ridge just ahead of him. From that same ridge another vulture dropped, descending in ever narrowing circles until it disappeared behind a wall to Longarm's right. Longarm pulled his black to a halt and studied the remaining vultures still in view.

The two birds had reached the brow of the ridge by this time, and though one of them immediately waddled out of sight, the other remained visible. Though it was better than six or seven hundred yards above the floor of the canyon, even at that distance Longarm could see the second bird's distended stomach and its hooked beak gleaming wetly in the sun. These birds were feeding on fresh carrion.

That was when Longarm thought of Cal Swinnerton.

Leaving the game trail, Longarm rode closer to the wall of rock, looking for an opening or trail through it to the other side. He rode on for more than half a mile before finding a narrow stream trickling through a cleft in the rock. Dismounting, Longarm tied the black's reins to a small pine, then clambered up through the icy stream to the floor of the arroyo. The swift water piled stiffly against his boots, threatening to sweep his feet out from under him at times, but he followed the stream deeper and deeper into the rock.

A few hundred feet along, the arroyo widened and Longarm rounded a shoulder of rock and found himself at the foot of a waterfall. The water was plunging from such a height that the fall resembled a shifting, misty spray by the time it reached the floor of the chasm. The rocks all around were black with moisture, and the chill of the place was delicious after the dry, baking sunlight of the trail. For a moment Longarm stood under the waterfall, his face lifted to its cool shower.

Then he looked around for another passage out of the place and found it in a narrow trail that lifted steeply to a draw beyond. As he proceeded through the draw, he found himself surrounded by immense, smooth-textured columns of rock. Threading his way past them, he came to another narrow trail that took him at last to the edge of a small, grassy meadow. He was through the rock wall.

He looked up. The vultures were still there, hanging above him in the sky. He watched, waiting for one of them to drop. At last the closest one, circling lazily, began its descent. As Longarm watched, the big bird disappeared into a narrow fissure in the rock face just ahead of him.

Longarm swore. It would not be an easy task for him to get into that fissure. But he had come this far. He walked over to the rock face and, using what niches and cracks afforded him purchase, climbed up the wall until he was able to pull himself into the narrow defile and follow it around a sharp bend.

Cal Swinnerton—or what was left of him—was wedged into a rocky cleft about ten feet above Longarm's head. Strips of clothing hung from the nearly clean skeleton. The vulture Longarm had followed was perched on Cal's skull, its hooked beak tearing into the tiny shreds of meat that still clung to the shoulder bone. A second vulture darkened the sky above Longarm's head before coming to rest on a narrow ledge close to Cal's feet. Without a glance at the first vulture, this one began tearing at what was left of Cal's boots. Both birds were too busy, it seemed, to note Longarm's presence.

Longarm held his handkerchief up to his face to protect him from the powerful stench that still emanated from the corpse. He edged closer, waving an arm to dislodge the feeding birds. Reluctantly, they spread their enormous wings and lifted from the body. With their monstrous shadows still hovering over him, Longarm climbed up the rough wall until he was on a level with Cal's remains.

There was nothing left of the face except the bone structure and the remains of one eye that stared dustily up at him. Reaching down, Longarm pushed back the remnants of the battered Stetson that had been jammed between the rock and the man's skull. A tuft of fair, sunny hair spilled from under it. He had been sure it was Cal before; now he was certain. Beaufort had described Cal Swinnerton as a towhead.

Dizzy from the stench, Longarm moved back and looked up the wall of rock at the narrow window of blue sky high above him. He might have been at the bottom of a well. From the look of Swinnerton's shattered body, there was no doubt he had been either thrown or pushed from the ridge above. There was no other way to explain the body's presence in this narrow defile.

Leaning back as far as he could, Longarm peered still closer at the ridge. Yes, it was the tip of a pine he saw. There was not just rock up there, but a trail as well—and Swinnerton must have been riding along it.

Turning about, he left Swinnerton's remains behind him and climbed back down to the grassy sward he had just left. Then he looked about him for some route that would take him to that trail above Swinnerton's body. His eye finally picked out a possible route. He would have to go all the way on foot, however, and then hope that the trail he found would lead him back to the canyon floor on the other side, where he had left his black.

It was a treacherous and difficult climb, and it left him winded. But when he reached the ridge, he realized he had found what he had been searching for. The hoofprints of two horses were clearly visible on the narrow trail. Longarm went down on one knee to inspect the prints. The horse on the outside, closer to the edge, was missing a shoe. That would be Swinnerton's gelding. The hoof was not yet split. That must have come later, Longarm realized, on the long, rough ride back to Landusky. And it was the right front foreleg—to settle it conclusively.

Moving carefully along the trail, he read the tracks and winced. As he had suspected, just before the spot where Cal Swinnerton's broken body lay, he could see where the rider behind Swinnerton had moved his mount in between the rock wall and the edge of the trail. The tracks were eloquent after that. It was not difficult to imagine Finn Larson pushing or striking out at Cal Swinnerton, sending him pitching out of the saddle and over the edge. Longarm could almost hear the horse's hoofs scrabbling and its frantic whinnying as it struggled to keep from being pulled over the edge after its unfortunate rider.

From that point on, Swinnerton's mount had galloped on alone, and the remaining horseman had turned around and gone back the way he had come. This set of tracks was the clearest.

And this second horseman, Longarm had no doubt, was Finn Larson.

Longarm started down the trail, following the gelding's tracks. They would lead him, he hoped, back to the canyon floor. Once there, he planned to return for his black, then ride back up here to this second set of hoofprints. It would mean a lot of walking, but that didn't matter. For he was certain he would find Finn Larson when he reached the end of that second trail of hoofprints.

The trail's descent from the ridge was gradual, and Longarm came out more than two hours later behind a compact stand of scrub pine. The stand was some distance from the canyon where the Deer River emerged from the mountains. It was an even longer walk back along the river to the spot where he had left his black.

Mounting it wearily, he rode back to the pines, then followed the trail onto the ridge and past the narrow path where Cal Swinnerton had gone over. From then on he followed the second rider's tracks. He was fortunate that it had not rained in more than a week. The horse's prints were still reasonably fresh, with only a few filled completely by blown sand.

The trail followed the crest of the ridge, which shouldered higher and higher, affording Longarm a spectacular view of the mountain range. Far to his right, the gleaming band of silver that was the Deer River wound its way through the range, and beyond it—on the other side of Bridger Peak—gleamed the blue cup of water that was Deer Lake.

To his left, Longarm saw only badlands, peaks, and ravines, with Horsehead looming over it all. From this angle the peak no longer resembled the head of a horse, but it dominated the landscape completely. And then Longarm was noting the trail ahead of him. It appeared to drop out of sight.

Pulling up, Longarm studied the trail closely, then gently coaxed his horse to the lip of ridge. As soon as he did so, he found it again swinging off to his left, winding close around a huge boulder. The trail dropped swiftly then, almost too steeply, before leveling off. Carefully, he urged his skittish black on past the boulder.

That was when Longarm glimpsed a green land far below, surrounded on all sides by precipitous cliffs.

Then, just as abruptly, the jutting fingers of rock closed off his view of the valley. But he knew now where he was heading: into a valley that only a rider with a map—or a fresh pair of tracks to follow—could have found.

Keeping on, Longarm followed the trail for another mile at least. Then, to his surprise, he found the trail ahead of him vanishing on a smooth rocky ledge that had nothing beyond it but a swift mountain stream piling headlong between two smooth walls of rock. He backtracked. There was no sign of the rider pulling off the trail before he reached the ledge. And there was no other set of tracks going back up the trail.

Longarm nudged the black off the ledge and into the stream bed, urging it on down through the damp cavern for better than a mile, the swift water piling up around the black's legs almost to its belly. At last the canyon's walls widened. Longarm rode out of the stream and found nothing to follow—no sign of Finn Larson's trail.

Furthermore, he was well beyond that valley he had glimpsed from the trail. He rode on for a mile or so further and found himself riding into a wide pass, one of the few that led through the range. Having spotted no further sign of Larson's tracks, he turned back to the stream.

As he rode back up through the rushing water this time, he carefully examined the sheer canyon walls on both sides. Less than a mile further on, he caught sight of a slight fold in the rock, behind which he glimpsed a narrow trail. He rode into it and soon found himself in a winding draw which only grudgingly allowed his horse passage through it. Presently Longarm came out onto a grassy sward on a ledge overlooking the valley he had seen from above.

How many hidden valleys such as this existed in these mountains, Longarm could only guess. But he was lucky to have found this one, he realized. It was even less accessible than the valley where he had taken Burt Williams.

Longarm took a quick look around. It was late in the

afternoon, but he had plenty of sunlight left. Dismounting, he began to lead his black into the valley. There was no sense in giving Finn Larson too fat a target.

Finn left the bank of the stream and started back through the pines, a string of four fat mountain perch dangling from his tackle. Finn Larson was content.

It had been seven years since he had discovered this remote roost high in the Deer River range. He had been forced to shoot his crippled mount and take refuge in a clump of pines outside the range on the crest of a foothill. When the posse that was after him at the time continued to press him, he had found the trail leading to the ridge. Later that same day, while looking for a campsite, he had discovered the valley.

The moment he entered the valley, he had felt a profound sense of peace. Its beauty seemed incredible, but even more awesome was its splendid, pristine isolation. No other white man had ever set foot on this soil, drunk from these icy streams, or moved through the deep, fragrant pines, alive then at twilight with the song of birds. When at last he came to the mountain lake and looked into its still, profound depths, he knew he had found the perfect place, an Eden he could claim as his own.

From a filthy sod shack in Minnesota where the vermin had free passage over the floors, the sink, the kitchen table, and over his restlessly tossing body at night, Finn Larson had fled westward at the age of fifteen, certain that his slattern of a mother and his puking drunk of a father would hardly give his absence a thought. He left them filled with a desire for something better—and a black rage he made no effort to control. Word of the mountain men had come to him as he grew up, but he was almost thirty years too late. The fur trade had destroyed itself by trapping the beaver

114

almost to extinction. Even the buffalo were gone.

All that was left of the West he had read about in dime novels were the lawless towns, the mindless killings, the painted women, and the liquor. It wasn't long before his temper got him into a shooting, and before he was eighteen he had killed his first man. The brutal finality of his act satisfied something deep within him, and soon he was riding with a gang eager for his easy willingness to kill.

With the money these depradations provided, Finn was able at last to buy himself a woman and, even more important, his brace of revolvers. For a while he was content. But only for a while. He could not last long with any gang, he soon found. He hated too easily and too deeply. And soon the smell of his companions sickened him—the old rage would rise like bitter gall to choke in his throat and he would move on, not always peacefully.

Then he found this valley. From that moment on, Finn had a purpose—to build in the valley and make it his own. Here he would be free from the stench of humanity. Here he would live with a woman of his own, one he did not have to pay for each time or relinquish within a few minutes to the next customer.

So had had joined the Warners. And after each successful raid, he had taken his share and ridden back to this valley, where he continued to build, returning to the Warners only when he needed more cash to continue the work on his place.

Now, as he emerged from the pines and smelled the sharp tang of the wood smoke issuing from his cabin's chimney, he felt again that exhilaration that fell over him whenever he realized that at last he was rid of towns and cities.

The pungent smell of wood smoke increased as he neared the cabin. Ellen had his supper on. That thought brought a smile to the pale sheen of his face. The woman was coming around, finally. Though she sure as hell protested when he took her, at the same time she had never come after him with a knife, the way his mother used to go after his father. Ellen liked him well enough, Finn had long since concluded. The more brutal he was when he took her, it seemed, the more violent were her climaxes. Hell, he knew what a woman wanted. A man who knew how to handle her. Not that it made any difference much what she wanted. It was what he wanted—his needs—that mattered. Besides, he would suspect her if he found her sucking around him like so many women he had known. He liked his women to hate him some. It added a spice to the relationship. He would have no respect for a woman otherwise.

He reached the cabin. Holding the string of perch away from his deerskin legging, he leaned his fishing pole against the side of it, opened the door, and stepped in.

Watching through the window as Finn approached the cabin, Ellen's resolve almost deserted her.

For more than an hour she had been waiting for Finn's return, cursing him for his delay and at the same time praying that he would not come back at all—that some blind stroke of fate would strike him down, ridding her of him forever. But of course it was not to be that simple—a fact that flooded over her with demoralizing impact the moment she caught sight of Finn's lean frame emerging from the pines, the gleaming perch dangling from his grasp.

The panic had passed by now, however, and she tightened her grip on the large carving knife she had sharpened especially for this deed. Flattening herself against the wall alongside the door, she heard Finn lean his fishing pole against the side of the cabin, then watched as the door swung open. She raised the knife over her head as Finn's lean frame filled the open doorway.

116

Finn stepped inside, the string of fish held out carefully before him. Closing her eyes, Ellen brought her knife down in a furious, slashing arc. But Finn had caught the movement out of the corner of his eye and was turning to face her, flinging his right arm up, when the knife struck. Ellen felt the knife catch something, but the blade did not penetrate — and at the same time her hand was struck with a powerful blow and the knife went flying.

Ellen opened her eyes as Finn grabbed her wrists and yanked her toward him. He dropped the string of perch and her bare feet slipped on one of the fish. She lost her footing. As she stumbled backward, Finn caught her up in his arms and, with a snarl, carried her across the floor toward the bed.

When she realized his intention, it drove her wild. She began beating him with her fists as she had done so often before. But, as usual, it did her no good. Her blows only seemed to increase his lust.

He flung her down onto the bed. The straw-filled mattress caught her in the small of her back and she felt the breath explode from her lungs. She tried to roll aside, but he was too quick for her. He pinned both her arms and dropped onto her. But she refused to give in and struggled with a deadly, silent intensity.

But Finn only seemed to grow stronger. Breathing heavily from the exertion, he grinned down at her. As usual, the man was enjoying himself immensely, she realized. Sweat from his face dropped onto her exposed breasts. It chilled her to the bone and made her struggle all the harder. Finn grunted in pain as her right hand, frozen into a claw, raked down the side of his face. He sat back quickly, measured her calmly, then sent his right fist crashing into her jaw.

For a moment she saw only bright pinpricks of light. The

bed seemed to lift under her. But she did not lose consciousness, and as Finn leaned close once again to take her, she pulled his arm close and sank her teeth into the sweaty, grimy, flesh. The taste of it nauseated her, but she hung on grimly despite Finn's shrill cry of pain. With his free hand he struck Ellen again, this time on the side of the face. It only caused her to bite deeper. The salty warmth of his blood filled her mouth. She felt it streaming down her chin as he swiped desperately at her face again and again.

At last, one shuddering blow fogged her resolve. She felt her jaws slacken. Another blow, equally powerful, caused her to release him. Still groggy, she got to her feet and tried to flee the cabin. But Finn was after her instantly. Overtaking her, he grabbed the back of her dress and with one swift downward yank, ripped it open to the waist.

Ellen screamed shrilly, then kicked out at Finn. But he yanked again and she stood before him naked. Still groggy, she tried to make it to the door, but he grabbed her shoulder and spun her around to face him. She tried to lift her arms up to protect herself, but she was not in time. Finn punched her repeatedly in the face, measuring each blow with merciless precision.

At last she collapsed forward into his arms. He caught her and carried her back to the bed. She tried not to respond as he entered her. Biting her lip in fury, she withdrew deep within herself, became an uninvolved spectator, ignoring at last his lusty cry of triumph as he climaxed. He rolled off her, and only then did she allow herself to cry. Powerful, racking sobs exploded from deep within her.

Longarm had heard the noise of the struggle inside the cabin twenty yards away. Having left his horse in a stand of pines, he was coming up on the cabin from the side. The front door must have been left open, he realized. Minutes before,

118

Finn's loud cry and then the woman's had come to him clearly. Now she was sobbing, filling the high, clean air around the cabin with the sound of her pitiful lament.

Despite himself, Longarm was unnerved by the woman's sobs. So he moved less cautiously than he otherwise would have as he turned the corner of the cabin and approached the open door. The late afternoon sun shone into his eyes, momentarily blinding him as he reached the doorway, his Colt out, and peered into the dim, shadowed interior of the cabin.

The woman had stopped crying now, and he thought he saw two people—one of them a naked woman, the other a fully clothed male—lying on a cot against the far wall. They appeared to be asleep.

He stepped cautiously into the cabin.

His left arm bleeding steadily where Ellen had bitten him, Finn was lying on the cot beside Ellen, his eyes barely open, a delicious drowsiness falling over him. Now that Ellen had stopped sobbing, he was close to sleep.

Suddenly the doorway darkened and a tall man with a Colt in his hand stepped into the cabin. He seemed to be having trouble peering into its dim interior, but he was looking directly at Finn and Ellen on the cot.

At once Finn knew who it was.—that crazy sonofabitch on the train. Longarm!

Finn reached down and snatched up the knife Ellen had tried to use on him. He grabbed Ellen's hair and dragged her around in front of him, shoving the point of the knife against her throat just under the chin. So incredibly swift was he that Ellen could only gasp in surprise as the knife dug into her flesh. Jumping up, Finn hauled Ellen to her feet also, keeping her in front of him, the blade still at her throat.

"Drop it, Longarm!" Finn cried. "Drop that iron or I'll sink this blade all the way!"

Desperately, Ellen tried to twist away. But Finn flung his bloody arm about her shoulders and, keeping her pathetic nakedness between him and Longarm, sank the knife deeper into her throat.

Longarm hesitated for only an instant. Despite the lack of light in the cabin, he could clearly see the bright tracery of the woman's blood as it streamed down her neck and across one breast.

He dropped his Colt to the floor.

Finn flung the girl from him, strode quickly forward, and picked up Longarm's Colt. He smiled as he backed up, the Colt trained on Longarm.

"Don't have a loaded revolver handy," he said by way of explanation. "Can't leave one about with this woman here. She might use it on me."

"I can't understand why," Longarm commented dryly. He glanced at the woman. She was slumped on the cot, her head down, the blood still seeping from the wound in her neck, streaking her naked breasts and torso garishly. She looked like hell.

"So you got here after all," Finn said. "Guess that means you took care of Seth and Luke. Well, now it's my turn, Long. I thought I'd finished you on the train, but I'll make sure this time."

He lifted the .44 carefully and sighted along its barrel.

Longarm had seen the girl out of the corner of his eye as she darted from the cot. Now Finn saw her as well. Startled, his face twisted in fury, he swung about to face her. That was when Longarm lunged for him. He caught the man waist-high and drove him back; but somehow Finn managed to stay upright as he slammed into the wall.

With measured fury, he clubbed Longarm viciously on

120

the head and shoulders. His skull was still sensitive from his earlier beating from the same man, and Longarm felt an explosion of disabling pain from deep within his head and found himself falling into semiconsciousness. His limbs went dead on him.

Chuckling aloud, doing his best to ignore the woman who was tearing at him viciously with her claw-like fingers, Finn continued to slash down at Longarm. At last, as one of the woman's nails caught Finn in the eye, he flung Longarm from him and turned on her with a furious cry of rage.

Barely conscious, his sight distorted by the veil of blood seeping down over his face, Longarm watched in helpless horror as Finn advanced on the woman, beating her about the head and shoulders with Longarm's Colt. At last, backed into a corner, she slid down the wall to the floor, uttering tiny, shrill cries of pain.

But still Finn went after her. The woman rolled over onto her stomach and covered her head with her arms. But Finn was beside himself now, and he continued to flail away at her with the Colt's barrel. His breath was coming in sharp, agonized bursts. He sounded like a man running full tilt up a mountain side.

And still—mindlessly—he continued to beat upon her unresisting nakedness. It was obvious to Longarm that he would soon kill her if he hadn't already. The monstrous, killing beast that dwelt within him was free now, and utterly without restraint.

With an enormous effort of will, Longarm reached down and pulled his derringer from his vest pocket. The effort it took to bring it out and cock one of the barrels caused sweat to stand out on his bloody forehead. But he managed. With his left hand he brushed the blood out of his eyes, aimed at Finn's back, and fired.

The roar sounded distant in his ears and he barely felt

the small pistol kick in his hand. But Finn spun about and went slamming back against the wall. He looked at Longarm with shock and horror. Blood was flowing from a wound in his left side. Leaning crookedly against the wall, he brought up Longarm's Colt and fired at Longarm. The round missed. Firing a second time, he was even wilder. It was obvious that Finn was in such pain he could not aim properly.

"I got one more shot!" Longarm heard himself shout. "Drop that gun!"

A twisted snarl on his face, Finn ignored Longarm's command. Using both hands to steady his aim, he raised the Colt to fire again. Before he could tighten his finger on the trigger, however, the woman, crumpled on the floor under him, reached a bloody hand up and grabbed the weapon, twisting it from his hand.

With a cry of rage, Finn turned and dove for the cabin door. He struck the doorjamb in his haste, then flung himself out crookedly and disappeared. Longarm heard him staggering across the yard, and a moment later the sound of his horse as he galloped away.

He put his head down gratefully. He had been unable to raise the derringer a second time, let alone cock it. The woman had saved him twice. He tried to turn his head to look in her direction, but before he could, the pistol fell from his hand and he sank into darkness.

Chapter 8

By the time Finn Larson reached Deer River, he was in trouble and knew it. He was unable to stanch the blood that pulsed from the hole in his side. The bullet had ripped on through, but it had torn out considerable muscle, and there seemed no way for him to stop the bleeding.

What kept him going was the rage smoking through his brain—rage at Ellen for her part in ruining his chance to kill that sonofabitch, and rage at Seth and Luke Warner. Finn had killed Swinnerton to keep his place hidden, so that meant it had to have been Seth or Luke who told the bastard how to get to his place. Longarm must have beaten it out of them before he killed them. Riding through the night, Finn found himself imagining how easy it must have been for that lawman to get those two no-accounts to blab. Perhaps they were still alive, after all—and had paid for their lives with the directions to Finn's valley.

Finn could not know any of this for sure. But for him, to suspect a thing was to believe it—and the thought of

123

Ellen's and the Warners' treachery burned within him. He would live, he swore, and he would finish off Ellen first. Then he would see to it that when he got done with them, Seth and Luke Warner would be cursing their mother for giving them birth. Better for them to have died at Longarm's hands than his.

Thoughts of Ellen intruded. His rage at her subsided somewhat, confusing him. Maybe he wouldn't kill her. Perhaps that would be better. He would give her another chance. He would bring her back to his valley, seal off the entrance with dynamite, and she would be his prisoner for as long as both of them lived. Once she realized there was no way out of his valley, she would accept the fact there was no one else for her. He would be patient with her. He would not cuff her unless she came at him. And soon she would glory in his lust for her. In time, he would make her weep and beg for him to take her.

In sight of Turley's place at last, Finn tried to pull up. Instead, he pitched sideways off his horse. Dazedly, he looked up at the evening sky. It came to him then that he had ridden all night and most of the day. No wonder he was so tired. The grass held him with a soft gentleness he had never known before. The earth was like a gently rocking cradle lulling him into a delicious sleep.

Only he must not sleep. He had things to do, vows he had promised himself to keep before that other long sleep came. He became dimly aware that the grass under him was becoming slick with his blood.

He closed his eyes to stop the universe from spinning . . .

When he opened them again, it was night. A wilderness of stars spanned the heavens. His horse was quietly cropping the grass at his head. As he reached out for its reins, the horse drew back quickly, snorting and shaking its head.

Patiently, Finn waited until the horse returned to cropping the grass beside his head before he reached out a second time. He caught hold of the reins this time and hung on as the horse shied back. When the horse quieted finally, Finn pulled himself to his feet. Once he was upright, he leaned heavily on the horse.

He could see light in the windows of the ranch building less than half a mile further on—the spread Rob Turley and his woman had bought. They would have to take him in. If he made it there.

He kept leaning against the horse, his hand on the saddlehorn. At last he thought he had gathered enough strength to pull himself into the saddle. He lifted his left foot and fitted it patiently into the stirrup. He tried to pull himself up and got about halfway before he slid down again.

He waited and rested a minute longer. Then he tried again. The third time he made it, dragging his right leg painfully across the cantle. He did not try to fit his foot into the stirrup. Once in the saddle, he took a deep breath and urged his horse toward the windows gleaming in the distance.

He rode sagged over the saddlehorn, clutching it with his right hand. The blood pulsing out of his side had caused his leg to grow as heavy as a tree limb. At times he felt the weight of it would pull him off the horse. But he kept on until he reached the front yard of the Turley spread, at which point his mount pulled up abruptly.

Finn lost his balance and toppled forward off the horse, piling limply onto the ground. The horse shied away from him, blowing nervously. Finn tried to call out to Rob, but little more than a groan came out. He was surprised at how dry his mouth was. He got up onto his knees and reached out for the horse, but he misjudged the distance and struck it on the nose. The animal spooked and, uttering a startled whinny, bolted away from Finn and out of the yard. Finn collapsed forward onto the cool grass and rolled over onto his back. The universe once again spun dizzily about him.

As the thudding hooves of the fleeing horse faded into the night, the door to the ranch house opened. A bright splash of yellow light flooded across the grass. Finn heard footsteps in the grass close by his head and closed his eyes wearily. It had become too much of an effort for him to keep them open any longer. Through the closed lids he could see the light from a lantern held just above him.

He heard Rob Turley's voice. "Jesus Christ! Talk about the devil! It's Finn Larson!"

The lantern leaned still closer, a sun trying to break through his lids. "He's been shot," said Wilma Reed.

"How long do you think he's been here?" Rob asked anxiously.

"I told you. I just heard a horse riding off. He must've just got here."

"He looks pretty bad."

The light and heat from the lantern moved down Finn's body. He wanted to say something, but was too exhausted to form the words. He had never realized before this time what an effort of will was required simply to speak.

"Leave him here, Rob," Finn heard Wilma plea. "Let him be. He'll be dead in the morning. Look at the grass under him. He's bleeding like a stuck pig."

"Think we should?" Rob sounded like all he needed was a little more convincing—and like he was hoping his woman would provide it.

"You remember that time in Pecos City, Rob, when you and Kid Curry were on that job in Billings?"

"Yeah. What about it?"

"This bloody sonofabitch took me, damn him. And he wasn't very polite about it, either. He told me if I ever told

126

you what he done, he'd kill the both of us. And I believed the sonofabitch."

Finn heard Rob's gasp of rage, then sighed wearily and opened his eyes, pulling his Bowie from his belt. He forced himself to smile.

"Help me in, you two," he told them, his voice a harsh whisper, "or I'll carve you up for crow bait. Then we can all three bleed to death out here."

Such was the terror that Finn Larson had been able to generate in those who knew him over the years that Turley and his woman made no effort to wrest the huge knife from Finn's grasp.

"Hell, Finn!" Rob protested. "No need to talk like that. We wouldn't leave you out here."

"Bullshit," Finn rasped, his voice so laced with contempt that Rob and his woman visibly wilted. "Now help me inside!"

Rob took Finn's shoulders, Wilma his arm, and together they pulled Finn to his feet. The pain was so excruciating when he began to walk that it acted as a goad that drove him on relentlessly into the ranch house. Their eagerness to placate him was balm as well. The power his willingness to punish gave him was an asset he was determined to exploit to the full.

No sir, Wilma hadn't liked it that time. But *he* sure as hell had. And he had known she would never forget it. The thought of how she had been that time sent the blood coursing through his limbs, warming him, banishing the chill of death that had played about him for a moment out there on the grass.

As they set him down on a couch in the corner of the big room next to the huge fireplace, he told Rob, "Get some packing to stop this bleeding. Then I'd like some coffee and grub. I could eat a bear."

As he watched Rob hurry off and saw Wilma head for the stove, he chuckled meanly to himself. Turley and the bitch had been going to let him lie out there and bleed to death. Well, goddammit, he would sure as hell do his best to make them wish they had done just that.

Longarm opened his eyes. He was facing a window. Beneath it was a sink. A wooden bucket was sitting beside it on the counter with a dipper handle sticking out of it. The window was covered with grime. But a bright, dazzling light managed to filter through it. It must be midday, Longarm realized.

He moved his head. The protest from within was immediate. A blinding pain caused him to groan slightly and his vision to fade momentarily. Reaching his hand cautiously up to his head, he found that it was swathed in bandages. Breathing carefully, he waited for the pain to subside and peered at the woman lying asleep on the dirt floor beside his cot, her cheek resting on her forearm.

A bloodstained bandage had been wrapped clumsily about the top of her head. Long, shoulder-length curls of auburn hair spilled out from under it. The right side of her face—the side facing up—was swollen and discolored, the skin around the eye puffy and shiny. She was wearing a dance hall skirt, black with red spangles, and a low-cut blouse. Its thin black straps cut into the pale flesh of her shoulders.

Turning his head very carefully, he looked out through the cabin's open door. What he saw filled him with a sudden realization of how good it was that he was still alive. Standing out clearly in the bright rays of the noontime sun, a large mule deer was cropping the lush grass. It was a doe. Her black-tipped tail was tucked away as she foraged. As he watched her, she raised her head alertly, her large ears testing the air.

Closer still, almost within the shadow of the cabin, an enormous jackrabbit was sitting on its haunches peering into the cabin, its nose quivering, its long ears standing straight up at attention. Rangy animal though it was, it must still have weighed close to seven pounds. Abruptly it turned around, showed its impudent back to Longarm, and commenced feeding on the grass in front of the cabin.

Watching the animals, Longarm realized that he and the girl must have been lying in this cabin as silent as death for some time. Otherwise, these wild creatures would not have dared venture this close to it. Could the woman be dead? he wondered in sudden alarm. He turned his attention back to her and looked more closely at her reclining form, and was reassured to see the steady rise and fall of her breast as she slept.

He braced himself carefully and sat up. The exertion made his head spin and increased tenfold the sloshing pain in his skull. As he started to get to his feet, the bed creaked under him. At once the woman on the floor came awake. She sat up in alarm and stared at him.

"Oh!" she cried. "You're awake!"

Her words alerted the jackrabbit and the mule deer. They vanished from sight in a twinkling. He smiled carefully down at her.

"Yes," he said, "I'm awake. How are you feeling?"

"I'm still sore some. Is your head all right?"

"I have a mean headache. But I've had that before. How long have I been out?"

"Two days, about. You were out of your head for some of it. Finn beat you about the head something awful, and it was swollen and broken through in places. I bathed it with cold water whenever you let me get near you."

"I'm sorry. I don't remember any of it."

"That's all right. I understand. Once when Finn beat me on the head I was off my nut for a time. Finn said it was funny, the way I acted. But I didn't laugh much when he told me."

"What's your name?"

She hesitated a moment, then got slowly and painfully to her feet. "Ellen," she told him.

Longarm was startled. He looked more closely at the woman and saw at once the resemblance to Laura Miller. Despite the bruises, her features were remarkably similar to those of her sister.

"And are you Finn's woman?"

"I guess you might say that. He bought me, fair and square. But I don't want to talk about it." Her eyes narrowed. "Are you a lawman?"

"Yes, but I have no warrant for Finn. I'm after him on my own."

"Do you have a name?"

"Custis Long. My friends call me Longarm."

She nodded. "You looked at me kinda strange when I told you my name."

"Did I? I'm sorry. This headache makes me squint some."

She relaxed. "You must be hungry."

"Yes, as a matter of fact, I am. Very hungry. I guess that's a good sign."

"I'll see what I can rustle up," she told him. "We don't have much variety, just a lot of salt pork, beans, and coffee."

"That'll be fine," he assured her.

Her saloon girl's dress was wildly out of place under these circumstances and gave her a sad, pathetic look as she limped over to the stove and began to build a fire. She seemed to be able to get around all right, but Finn had beaten her with a fury Longarm shuddered to recall; and there was an outside chance he might have caused permanent injury to her as he flailed away at her with the barrel of Longarm's Colt.

"You saved my life," he told her.

Without glancing over at him, she said, "I did it for myself as much as for you."

"Well, I owe you."

She turned to look at him then, and smiled. It must have hurt her, so swollen and misshapen was her face. "You don't have to feel that way," she told him. "I'm glad I was able to help."

"How do you feel?"

"I'm all right. I thought he broke some bones, at first. It's just my back that hurts now—and it's getting better."

As he watched her prepare his meal, he realized that he had found Bill Miller's daughter. There could be no doubt of that. The resemblance to her sister along with the fact of her first name was proof enough. It only remained for him to tell her that her father and sister were in the area looking for her—anxious to give her a home again.

The question was, did Ellen want that home? Was she too ashamed? Would she light out rather than have her father find her like this? Would she be able to stand the questions she would see in her father's eyes, and in Laura's too?

But she had a right to know they were here and to make that decision for herself. Longarm decided he would bring the matter up after they had eaten. He was not looking forward to it.

It was Ellen's idea that they eat outside the cabin, which was getting quite warm from the heat of the day and the fire roaring in the stove. She helped him drag the mattress out of the cabin. Together, they settled on a grassy sward

131

behind the cabin near the pines. It was almost like a picnic, the way she handled it. She seemed to be feeling and moving much better, and he no longer minded the garish outfit she had on when she explained to him that Finn had ripped her only other dress to shreds.

She seemed content as she brought out the food. Both of them were very hungry and ate in comparative silence. By the time Longarm had finished, his headache had subsided considerably, though he did not dare put his hand up to his head for fear of causing another explosion. And he still had to move very carefully. Once again, thanks to Finn Larson, he had suffered a severe concussion, if not a skull fracture.

After they finished the meal, she brought a large wooden tub out to the pump by the well, filled it with water, and proceeded to wash the dishes, using a bar of yellow soap and scrubbing them down thoroughly with a heavy brush. As she bent over the large wooden tub, her thick auburn curls fell forward and she was constantly having to brush them back again over her shoulders.

Longarm was strangely affected as he watched this woman working so diligently in the midst of this wilderness to clean a few dishes. Recalling what she must have suffered at the hands of Finn Larson, he wondered at her amazing recuperative powers. There was, he realized finally, a very simple explanation. No matter what the so-called good people of this earth would have to say on the matter of Ellen's past, she had great strength of character.

After she brought the clean dishes back into the cabin, she came back out and sat next to him on a camp stool.

She sat quietly, without a word, and Longarm was reluctant to break the peaceful stillness of the valley. In spite of the altitude, its climate was temperate. Longarm knew that remote valleys such as this often enjoyed milder weather than places lower down because of the protection afforded by the barrier of peaks on all sides. Finn Larson had been fortunate indeed to find himself such a haven. Longarm did not wonder at his eagerness to keep it hidden from the world.

At the thought of Larson, Longarm stirred restlessly and glanced at Ellen. She caught the glance and frowned.

"You been meaning to ask me something," she said. "Why don't you go ahead?"

"It's about Finn."

She took a deep breath. "What about him?"

"You said he had bought you, fair and square. What did you mean by that?"

"Just what I said." She gazed boldly at Longarm for a moment, then looked away, her eyes on the lake beyond the pines below the cabin. "I let myself get mixed up with a no-account. He made me a lot of promises and we ended up in Landusky just before the mines played out. He lit out, left me with nothing, not even a goodbye or a thank you, ma'am. And, of course, he left me without a cent."

Longarm nodded. How often, he wondered sadly, had he heard this story, or one similar to it, over the years. The things good people did to each other sometimes appalled him more than the lawless actions and killings of the criminals it was his business to track.

"So you had to go to work," he prompted gently.

"Yes—work. You see this dress I'm wearing, so you know what that meant. For three years I worked at the Silver Slipper. Then I got tired of it—tired of getting pawed and pushing drinks."

She stopped then and took a deep breath. It was clear that what came next was not something she was eager to relate. Longarm said nothing and waited patiently.

"So I went to work at Ma Ridley's place," she said, her

voice low. "Ma was good to me, as good as she knew how, that is." She shrugged. "It wasn't so bad. Not really. I got to sleep late in clean sheets. And I could usually choose who I went with. Then Finn began stopping in. He's a fearsome, violent man, and what he did to some of Ma's girls was a terrible thing to see."

"I have no doubt of that. How did he manage to buy you?"

"He had been terrifying Ma and the girls for weeks. He wasn't being very nice to me, either. But the more I fought him, the better he liked it. Pretty soon he told Ma he wanted to take me with him. Ma wouldn't let him, but I saw what her defiance was doing to her and the others, so I proposed to Finn that he buy me."

"For three hundred dollars, as I understand it."

She was startled. "You know?"

"I don't suppose there are many people in Landusky who don't know about Finn's remarkable purchase. What I would like to know is why you did it for Ma."

"Because Ma saved my life. Not long after I went to stay with her, I came down with diphtheria. I almost died. Ma and the girls nursed me through it. I owed them. Besides, I had the crazy idea that if I didn't like it with Finn, I could always leave him, take the money Ma was holding for me— that three hundred dollars Finn had given her for me—and leave this country." She laughed shortly, bitterly, and looked around at the cliffs hemming in the valley. "I didn't realize how difficult getting out of this place would be, or how impossible it would be for me to just up and walk out on Finn Larson."

"So you became his prisoner."

"That's about the size of it. I don't even know how to get out of this valley."

"You don't?"

134

She shook her head. "He blindfolded me when he took me into the mountains, and to make doubly sure, we entered the valley at night. I've tried to find the way out more than once."

Longarm could understand Ellen's difficulty. Once the trail from the ledge overlooking the valley reached the valley floor, it lost itself in a thick grove of pines, the thick mat of pine needles effectively wiping out any trace. Unless Ellen knew in which portion of the grove to look for it, she would never be able to find the trail by herself.

"Ellen," Longarm said, "you haven't told me your last name."

"I know that."

"Is it Miller?"

"Who told you?" she flared. "How did you know that?"

"Your sister Laura told me," Longarm replied.

"Laura!"

"She's here with your father. They've come here in hopes of finding you. Your father and Laura are settling along the Deer River in what looks like prime bottomland. Since you were last heard of in Landusky, he has come all this way to find you."

Her face had gone chalk-white as he spoke. For a moment she was too upset to say anything. Then, with tears streaming down her cheeks, she said, "Well, you're never going to take me to him, if that's your intention. He's never going to know what I've—what I've become."

"It's not my intention to take you anywhere, Ellen. That's not why I showed up in this valley. But I think you should think of your father and your sister. They have both come a long way to find you. They love you very much."

The woman broke down completely then. Holding her battered face in her hands, she sobbed as if her heart were being torn from her. It reminded Longarm of her heart-breaking cries when he was first approaching the cabin. He looked away, as affected by her crying now as he had been then.

At last she calmed down. Dabbing at her eyes with the bottom of her skirt, she asked Longarm to excuse her for the outburst. Then, her head back proudly, she asked, "How soon do you think it'll be before you can ride, Longarm?"

"Another day. Maybe two, at the most. I've had this kind of punishment before and I'm getting to know what my limits are."

"You'll take me out of here with you?"

"Of course."

"What about Finn? Suppose he comes back?"

"I'll kill him if he does, but I don't think that's likely. I'll have to keep after him."

"If he finds me, he'll kill me for helping you."

Longarm smiled. "For saving my life, you mean. But don't worry. He won't find you."

"Is—is there a price on Finn's head?" she asked hopefully.

"No."

She frowned. "Then why are you after him? You're a lawman, you said."

"A deputy U.S. marshal, Ellen," he told her. "But I'm not on assignment now. I have my own reasons for tracking—and killing—Finn Larson."

"Why?"

"Let's just say he needs killing."

"Yes," she agreed softly. "He does. He is a monster. I have never known a man so . . . so depraved—or one who so enjoyed giving pain to others. He does need killing, that's true. But . . . won't that make you a murderer?"

Longarm shrugged.

She shuddered and he saw her pull away from him. It

was barely noticeable, and she was probably unaware herself that she had done so. But Longarm noticed—and understood.

"I'm tired," he said to her. "Get me a blanket. I think I'll nap out here for a while."

She got up from the camp chair, reached over, and gently touched the bandage she had wrapped about his head. "I didn't mean to do that," she said. "It was just the way you said Finn needed killing. So—coldly."

"You don't need to explain, Ellen."

"I hate Finn Larson too. I tried to kill him just before you came. But you made it sound so . . . cold-blooded. It's like you've appointed yourself judge and jury and executioner all in one."

"Perhaps I have."

She looked at him a moment longer, then turned quickly and hurried toward the cabin to get the blanket he had requested.

Longarm pulled his own horse up to let Ellen ride on ahead. Miller had just stopped sawing a fence post and with shaded eyes was peering at the two of them as they rode closer. Laura was standing beside him. Ron Walker and Cynthia were some distance away in the front yard. Billy was standing with Beaufort in the cabin's open doorway.

Suddenly Ellen could contain herself no longer. Whipping Finn's old pack horse to a tired gallop, she cried out, "Father!" Longarm saw Bill throw down the saw. He and Laura rushed to meet Ellen as she flung herself from the horse and into her father's arms.

All during the ride from the valley, Ellen had been quiet and very apprehensive as to how her father would greet her. But now, Longarm noticed with great pleasure, all her apprehension had vanished, wiped away by her joy at seeing her father and sister again. The family was reunited, and nothing else mattered. Explanations would take care of themselves.

Though Longarm had said nothing to Ellen, so as not to worry her, he had not taken the journey well, even though he had spent an extra couple of days in the valley to regain his strength. Now, as he approached the happy group surrounding Ellen, he was keeping himself in the saddle only through sheer tenacity. His head was splitting. As he urged his black on, the reins felt like ropes in his hands, and the animal seemed bent on throwing him with each stride.

He rode slowly up to the happy gathering. By this time Beaufort, Billy, Ron Walker, and Cynthia were joining enthusiastically in the welcome. It was Beaufort who appeared to notice Longarm's condition first.

Hurrying over to him, the doctor looked up at Longarm, a concerned frown on his face. "You all right, Longarm? You look poorly."

"I feel poorly."

At that moment a very happy Bill Miller rushed over to Longarm. "You found her!" the man cried, vigorously pumping Longarm's hand. "I don't know how to thank you!"

Longarm managed a grin. "I've just been thanked. I saw the look on your face and on Ellen's. That's thanks enough. Now, would someone give me a hand getting off this horse before I fall off?"

As he spoke, he leaned forward and tried to pull his left leg over the cantle. But his head was swimming by that time, and he lost his bearings. All he remembered was the astonished Miller catching Longarm in his arms as he pitched forward off his horse. After Longarm assured a concerned Ellen that he would be all right, he allowed Beaufort and Ron Walker to help him toward the cabin.

"What happened, Longarm?" Beaufort asked.

"Got clubbed by Finn Larson. On the head. It's mighty damn sore."

"You have a concussion then. That can be very dangerous, Longarm. Maybe you should not have ridden so soon after. You're going to need rest."

"Yes, Doctor."

Beaufort grinned.

"You look hale and hearty," Longarm remarked as they entered the cabin's cool interior.

"Good food, lots of fresh air, and the love of a beautiful woman. Works every time."

"So I heard," Longarm said feebly as they let him down gently on the cot against the wall. Leaning his head back, he closed his eyes. It was as if someone had turned off the world as he sank at once into an exhausted, dreamless sleep.

Wilma Reed was just five feet four. Beside Rob Turley, she looked like a child. Her black hair was short and curly, and as she looked up into Rob's face, Turley saw tears gleaming in Wilma's gray eyes. It astonished him. Wilma was a tough woman, part Indian and part German. She rode better than most men and was probably a better rifle shot than Annie Oakley.

They were standing outside by the corral. The moon was high overhead, as bright as a new silver dollar. He could see its face clearly.

"What is it, Wilma? What's wrong?"

"Finn," she told him. "It's Finn. How long, Rob? How long is he going to stay with us?"

"Till he's better, I reckon. I can't just kick him out."

She reached out and clasped him about the waist, resting her face against his chest. "I know that," she said. "He'd kill you if you tried to."

"That's not it, Wilma," Rob said, pushing her away so he could look into her eyes. "You sayin' I'm afraid of Finn?"

"Of course you are! You'd be a fool not to be. And you're not a fool. It's like we're living in a cave with a rattlesnake that might strike any minute. I hate him, Rob. He makes me sick to my stomach. Every time I look at him and think of what he made me . . ." She shuddered and Rob quickly pulled her close to him and hugged her tightly.

Wilma was right, he realized. He *was* afraid of Finn. He just hadn't realized how upset Wilma was at the man's presence. She had seemed to take it all in stride. But then he reminded himself of how seldom she had smiled since Finn first set foot in their house—and how seldom either of them had been able to comfort the other in their bed at night.

He groaned inwardly at his frustration. He had thought of murdering Finn while he slept, but he could not bring himself to do it. The thought appalled him. To kill a man in the course of a robbery, during the heat of a chase or of a violent disagreement was one thing. But to kill in cold blood a man who was sleeping peacefully under his roof . . . !

No, Rob Turley was *not* a Finn Larson.

"How is that wound of his, Wilma?" he asked.

"Better. Didn't you see him out here today, practicing with that sixgun you gave him?"

"I saw him. He looked kinda pale."

She nodded. "But his wound has healed cleanly."

"So what's keeping him here?"

"I wish I knew, Rob. And I don't dare ask him."

"Me neither."

"And every time he looks at me with those burning eyes of his, or smiles at me . . ." She shuddered once again. "He's like some animal that lives in dark, unclean places."

140

She rested her head on his chest again. He patted her tight curls and tried to think of something to say. Then, looking past her at the ranch house, he saw Finn's figure loom in the open doorway, blocking out the bright yellow lantern light.

Rob said softly, "He's standing in the doorway now, watching us."

Wilma quickly stepped back from Rob. She did not look toward the ranch building. Abruptly, Finn left the doorway and disappeared back into the house.

"Just keeping an eye on us," Rob commented bitterly.

This was not the first time he and Wilma had tried to use the money they had stolen to buy a place and go straight—maybe even raise children and become respectable. The first time, up in Powder Springs, Wyoming Territory, things had gone sour when their old buddies showed up and began using their ranch as a hideout. Soon, Wilma and he had been drawn into a job, and that was the end of their dream.

He didn't want that to happen this time. But with Finn coming by like this—possibly drawing that U.S. marshal after him—Turley could see it all unravelling again.

Then he had a thought. "We need to get away from Finn," he told Wilma. "It'll give us a chance to think."

"But where can we go? Finn won't let us out of his sight. He's like a jailer."

"That house-raisin' down by the river—for that new sodbuster, Miller."

"What about it?"

"You remember. Zeke Bannister rode by yesterday to invite us to it."

"You mean you think we should go?"

"Sure, why not?"

"We're supposed to be ranchers. We've got cattle. These grangers are already taking the best quarter sections along the river."

"We were invited. No reason we can't be neighborly, is there? And it's a perfect excuse to get away from Finn for a while. Wouldn't you like that?"

"Do you think he'd let us go?"

"I'll tell Finn that I've already told Zeke I'd be proud to join the settlers along the river in their house-raisin', and so if I don't go, they might get suspicious. Hell, Wilma, it won't hurt to try."

For the first time in a long time, Wilma smiled. "Let's do it," she said. "And maybe when we come back he'll be gone!"

But as Turley put his arm around Wilma's waist and started back with her to the house, hr realized that her hope was a futile one at best. There was little likelihood that Finn Larson would be gone when they got back. But it might give them a chance to work something out.

Finn Larson had sure as hell worn out his welcome—not that any had ever been extended to him in the first place.

Chapter 9

On the day of the cabin-raising, Bill Miller had everything ready.

With Beaufort helping as much as his condition allowed—and it was clear to Longarm that he was getting stronger with each passing day—Bill Miller, his two daughters, and the Walkers had succeeded in clearing away the brush from the site where they planned to build. By this time, Miller and the others had already cut the logs and hauled them to the proper location on the site. The night before, Miller had just managed to finish hewing each log smooth with a broadax and fitting them with notches at the end so they would join securely at the corners.

Watching him that evening while he rested on a camp stool, Longarm could only marvel at Bill Miller's almost fierce capacity for work. Longarm's sympathies would always lie with the cattlemen, not with the nesters who sometimes seemed almost wanton in their eagerness to plow up sweet meadowlands and parks. But watching Bill Miller and the others labor throughout that day, he felt nothing but admiration for them. In sharp contrast to Finn Larson and those like him who stank up the West, these people represented hope and decency.

The other settlers along the river began arriving before daybreak. As Longarm kept in the cool shadows of the crude dugout where the Millers had been staying, the work began in earnest. Watching from the doorway, eager to keep out of everyone's way, Longarm watched as the men sent the logs up the skids, some pushing from below, others hauling on a rope from atop the slowly rising wall of logs. It was amazing how swiftly and expertly they cut the logs to fit around the windows and the doorway, and kept going.

Others worked on the barn and the corral and still others kept busy making rough-hewn tables and chairs and other furniture from the split logs Bill Miller had prepared. The cabin's floor, meanwhile, was being put down by a tall, bewhiskered fellow with a high-pitched voice whose specialty was this odd craft. When Longarm drifted over and watched how the man fitted the split logs together and smoothed them with his adze, the chips flying like a miniature snowstorm, he could only shake his head in admiration.

Just before the noon meal, with three sides of the cabin already up, two riders—a man and a woman—approached the gathering, greeted a few of the settlers, then dismounted. They had come to help also, it appeared, though it was soon obvious to Longarm that they were cattle raisers, not sodbusters, and had few useful talents for this particular undertaking.

But that was not what caught Longarm's attention.

It was the woman. She had ridden up beside her husband, the easy skill with which she rode making it virtually impossible to tell her from a man. She was dressed like a man and carried herself like a man. Recalling Burt Williams's description of Wilma Reed and Rob Turley, Longarm realized that he had unwittingly stumbled upon them. As he half expected, Williams had been lying when he maintained that the two of them had gone back to Texas.

Then this was where every member of the Warner gang had come to bury the stench of the past.

For the rest of the day, Longarm kept himself out of sight inside the dugout, while he maintained as close a surveillance as he could on the two ranchers. The woman he was sure was Wilma Reed—she was slightly built and considerably shorter than Turley—found work with the settlers' wives, preparing food to stoke the ravenous appetites of the furiously working men, all of whom, Longarm noticed, treated her with elaborate respect. Longarm wondered if this was because of her small slim figure or the gleaming sixgun strapped to her hip.

That night one of the men who had been building furniture all day produced a fiddle, and before long the entire company was square dancing in the light of lanterns hung from ropes stretched between the trees and the corner of the newly completed cabin. Not only was the cabin finished, but the barn as well. Both structures looked raw but sturdy in the lantern light. Longarm was astonished at the energy of the men and women responsible for this remarkable day's construction. They had been working like draft animals from the crack of dawn, and now they seemed determined to dance all night.

But at last they began to call to their children and climb into their wagons and flatbeds and start off through the night to their homesteads. Anxious to be free of his confinement, Longarm left the dugout then and, keeping to the shadows, moved closer to the small clusters of settlers that still remained.

One such group consisted of Bill Miller and his two daughters, who were in an animated conversation with Turley and Wilma Reed. Longarm held up and remained in the shadows as he waited for them to break up. As he watched, he saw that Ellen seemed quite familiar with Turley and his woman. It appeared that they were more than casual acquaintances.

When at last the two ranchers rode off, Longarm stepped out of the shadows and approached Miller and his two daughters. Beaufort came over to join them. At the sight of him, Laura took his arm and leaned her head against the frail doctor's shoulder.

"Hungry, Longarm?" Miller asked. "You must be famished, holed up like that all day."

"No, Bill," Longarm replied. "Ellen took care of that." He smiled at her as he spoke. "That last piece of rhubarb pie she sent in with Billy really hit the spot."

"I made it myself," Ellen said, her smile suddenly shy.

"It was sure good!" piped up Billy, as he joined them. "Longarm shared his second piece with me."

Longarm ran his hand through Billy's tousled head. "I took pity on him, Ellen. I'm sure you understand." Then Longarm looked sharply at Bill Miller. "Soon's you get a chance, I'd like a word with you, Bill."

Longarm's tone sobered all of them. Laura took Billy by the hand and, accompanied by the attentive Beaufort, took the protesting youngster over to where Cynthia and Ron Walker were preparing to get into their wagon. As soon as they were gone, Longarm turned to Ellen.

"Those two ranchers. You know them?"

"Yes. I met them when I worked in the Silver Slipper." Ellen spoke without hesitation and within earshot of her father.

146

Longarm glanced at Miller. "You know about Ellen working at the Silver Slipper?"

Miller nodded soberly. "Ellen has told me everything, Longarm. And I'm glad she has. She's afraid that Finn Larson will come after her if he is still alive. She wanted to warn me, and I'm glad she did."

Longarm nodded. He was pleased that Ellen had had the courage to be honest with her father and that the man had taken the news with as much understanding as he obviously had.

"Well, there's just one thing, Bill. Do you—or Ellen—have any idea who those two riders were?"

"The Smiths," Miller said with an ironic smile. "But whoever they are, they just bought the Double D ranch in the foothills, where the river curls north. They've got quite a spread, I understand. And it was right neighborly of them to stop by. You won't see many cattlemen helping out a granger like that. Seems like they'll make nice neighbors, and that's sure a comfort."

"Maybe so, Bill, maybe so. But I think those two are Rob Turley and Wilma Reed, members of the Warner gang. Long-standing sidekicks of Finn Larson."

Ellen gasped.

Longarm nodded grimly. "And I think there's a good chance that after Larson fled from that valley of his, he searched them two out. I think he might be staying at the Double D right now."

Miller swore softly and looked with quick alarm at Ellen. "Oh, my God, Ellen! Now Finn will know where you are!"

"What's this?" inquired Beaufort, as he and Laura rejoined them. "Did I hear you mention Finn Larson?"

"You did," responded Longarm. He looked back at Miller. "Exactly what *did* you tell Turley and his woman?"

"I told them Finn Larson was a madman. That he held Ellen prisoner in that valley of his. And I asked them to ask all the other ranchers to keep an eye out for him. I made it pretty damn clear that if I ever laid eyes on Finn Larson, I'd kill him."

"Strong words, Bill," said Beaufort.

"Well, I meant them!"

"If he's with them," said Longarm, "he'll get the message—and be on his way here for Ellen as soon as he can ride. If, that is, that wound I gave him didn't kill him."

"That's right," said Laura hopefully. "He might be dead."

"That's certainly a possibility," agreed Beaufort. "But a man like Finn Larson doesn't die easily."

"I agree," said Longarm.

"Oh, what are we going to do?" Ellen moaned. She was growing more distraught by the minute as she listened to the conversation. Longarm saw her begin to shiver, as if she had stepped into a sudden draft.

"I'm riding out tonight," Longarm told her. "Bill, if you'll help me saddle up—and if you'll pack some supplies for me, Ellen—I'll be on my way."

"Where are you going?" Ellen asked.

Longarm smiled coldly. "After Finn Larson."

"You don't have to do that," Miller said stoutly. "You've done enough for us already."

"This is my business as much as it is Ellen's," Longarm replied, "and I don't think we should talk on it much longer. Rob Turley and Wilma Reed are already a good stretch ahead of me."

"But you're still so weak," Ellen protested. "How can you ride?"

"I'm well enough to ride."

148

"I'm going with you, Longarm," said Beaufort.

"No, you're not," responded Longarm quickly. "I want you to stay here. I may not be able to stop Finn. If he gets past me, you'll be the only one between him and the Millers. I'm counting on you to stop him if I can't."

Beaufort hesitated for a moment, then nodded. "You can count on me, Longarm."

"Good," Longarm said.

Bill Miller started past Longarm toward the corral. "I'll get your horse," he said.

Ellen started to say something to Longarm, but evidently thought better of it. She turned quickly and hurried toward the dugout to pack Longarm's supplies.

It was well past midnight when Rob Turley crested the ridge overlooking his ranch and pulled his mount to a halt. As Wilma reined in her horse beside his, he continued to stare grimly down at his ranch house. Light was showing in the window. Finn Larson was there still, burning kerosene and waiting for their return. He was probably cleaning his sixgun at the moment—something he had been doing constantly for the past few days.

"What is it, Rob?" Wilma asked.

He looked at her and poked his hat back off his forehead. "I been thinkin'."

"About Finn?"

He nodded. "About Finn. And those nesters back there."

"You mean the Millers."

"Ellen Miller, especially."

She was the one Finn Larson wanted. Finn had told them about it often enough. How she had struck him from behind, then wrestled the gun from his hand, preventing him from killing that marshal. Finn wanted her back, not only to

149

punish her, but to return with her to that valley of his. It was all he talked about—when he talked. And now, by a lucky stroke, Rob and Wilma had found her.

Turley looked into Wilma's face, pale in the moonlight, and saw at once that she knew what he was thinking.

"I don't like it, Rob," she said softly.

"You think I like the idea? But hell, Wilma, we came away from here to figure a way to rid ourselves of Finn, didn't we? Can you think of a better way? Besides, didn't that Miller fellow give us a challenge to take to Finn if we found him? He said he'd kill Finn if he ever laid eyes on him. Hell, Wilma, maybe the sonofabitch will!"

Wilma snorted. "Finn'll eat him alive. You know that, Rob."

"Either way, it'll rid us of Finn Larson. If Miller kills him, we're all out of it. If Finn takes the woman back with him to that roost of his, we'll likely never see him again."

"You're forgetting one thing, Rob."

"You mean that U.S. marshal? No, I'm not. But he wasn't at that shindig as far as I could see."

"That don't prove nothing. He's around somewhere. I can feel it."

"Sure he's around. Looking for Finn Larson. And that's another damn good reason for sending Finn after Ellen Miller. If that guy's after Finn, we don't want Finn holing up with us."

She sighed and shook her head resignedly. "It's such a hell of a thing to do," she protested. "Sending that killer after the Millers. Makes me feel unclean."

"Okay, then," Turley said, clapping spurs to his mount and starting down the slope toward the ranch house. "We won't say a thing to Finn about Ellen Miller. After all, a guest like Finn Larson's a real joy to have around."

150

He heard Wilma's horse picking its way down the trail behind him and then her voice, sharp and decisive. "All right! Do it, Rob. Tell the sonofabitch. And then we'll both pray that Miller will take him."

He turned in his saddle and smiled bleakly through the darkness at Wilma. "That's right," he said. "We'll *both* pray."

Finn was sitting in a chair by the kerosene lamp, an oily cloth in his hand, the gleaming sixgun resting beside him on the table. Turley had been right. Finn Larson had been sitting here alone cleaning his sixgun while he waited for them to return. As the two strode in, Finn regarded them warily.

"Been gone some time," he remarked.

"Hell, Finn," said Turley. "We put up a cabin and a barn, complete with a corral. Then we did some real stomping. Best fiddler I heard in a long time. We're turning into real neighbors."

"Neighbors to a pack of nesters," Finn snarled. "How come you're so anxious to cozy up to them shit-kickers?"

"I told you," said Wilma. "It wouldn't have looked right if we hadn't gone. You know that, Finn."

"Shit!"

Finn plucked his sixgun off the table and hefted it, his eyes on both of them. He suspected them—of what, they could only guess. If there had been any doubt in either of their minds what to do, this greeting had taken care of that.

Turley cleared his throat. "I got news for you, Finn."

Finn was immediately suspicious. "News?" He glanced quickly at Wilma, then at Rob, as if he thought they were hatching some deadly conspiracy. And, of course, he was right. Wilma shuddered involuntarily and looked quickly

151

away from Finn's pale face, the icy, soul-less eyes.

"That's right," Turley hastened to add. "News. Don't you want to hear it?"

"Well, what's stoppin' you?"

"We found Ellen—that woman of yours."

Finn was on his feet in an instant. "You found her? Where?"

Regaining her composure, Wilma said, "She's the daughter of that nester we went to help today. She even told us you held her prisoner. She had no idea we knew you."

"A prisoner!" Finn cried. "I paid for her, by God! She's a liar!" His eyes narrowed warily. "You say she's with her father? Then where was that U.S. marshal?"

"We didn't see him nowhere, Finn," said Rob. "And they didn't mention him."

"She couldn't have got out of the valley without him. That means I didn't kill him. Damn!" Finn's eyes narrowed. "He'll be after you two, you know. It ain't just me he's after. It's all them that was part of that Glendale train robbery."

"We'll be ready for him, Finn."

"Sure you will."

Finn's face went cold, his blue eyes intent. "Well, the next time he comes after me, I'll be in my roost waitin' for him. But I sure as hell ain't goin' to wait for him alone." He reached for his gunbelt hanging on the back of the chair and buckled it around his waist. "I'm going out to saddle up," he told them. "I'll need some provisions."

Wilma nodded quickly.

Finn looked around the room. His eyes fell on Rob's sombrero and the poncho hanging on a wooden peg beside it. "I'll be needin' that sombrero and poncho, Rob. I can't ride without a hat, and I didn't take my jacket when I left my place. I was in too much of a hurry."

Turley tried not to hide his eagerness as he said, "You're welcome to it, Finn. Go ahead and take 'em both."

Finn grinned. He was enjoying himself immensely. "You two sure as hell are glad to be rid of ol' Finn, ain'tcha. Well, let me tell you, I want clear directions to this Miller place, and if Ellen ain't there like you say, I'll be back. That's a promise."

Then he strode from the cabin, disappearing into the darkness toward the stable. Finn wasn't even going to wait until daybreak before taking after that woman of his. But Turley didn't mind one bit.

He looked across the room at Wilma. She caught his glance.

"Thank God," she whispered.

The high, thin cry of a blackbird awakened Longarm. He opened his eyes and found himself looking up through the branches of the enormous pine tree under which he had camped. When he saw the pale light in the eastern sky, he cursed softly and sat up, peeling back the soogan. It was sopping wet from the pre-dawn dew. He stood up, shook it out, then rolled it hastily and packed it into his saddle roll.

He had not intended to sleep this late. He still had a considerable distance to travel through wooded foothills before he reached the Double D spread. But he had been almost completely exhausted by the time he got this far the night before, so he had concluded it would be a good idea to make camp until daybreak. Only it was past daybreak, and now, quite unhappy with himself, he decided against taking the time to build a fire and make breakfast.

He was lugging his saddle over to his black when he heard the click of a horseshoe against stone. The sound had come from the trail below him. Longarm put the saddle

153

down quickly and peered over the ridge. From far below him came the faint jingling of a bit and the steady clop of a horse's hooves. Longarm saw nothing, however, since that portion of the trail was well screened by a thick stand of mountain ash.

And then the rider emerged from cover.

It was a Mex. The sombrero he wore was a large one, and his poncho was very colorful. What a Mexican would be doing this far north, Longarm had no idea. But the rider was going toward the river, in the opposite direction Longarm was taking. Longarm watched the rider until he disappeared into another stand of mountain ash, then went back to his horse to saddle up.

The sun was peeking over a towering peak to his right when Longarm finally crested a ridge and found himself looking down at the Double D ranch. He had seen very little sign of beef on the Double D rangeland and was not surprised. Ranching was work. Rob Turley and Wilma Reed were ranchers in name only. As soon as their money ran out, they would return to their old ways of earning a livelihood.

The buildings were tucked into a loop of the river, hard against a foothill. Behind the buildings the Deer River range reared up massively and on both sides of the compound smaller foothills, heavily wooded, looked down upon the ranch.

Longarm touched his spurs to his black's flanks and followed the spine of the ridge further west, having decided to approach the ranch buildings from the northernmost foothill.

An hour later Longarm was sitting his horse in a thick stand of pine high above the ranch buildings on the crest of a ridge. He had been watching the ranch compound for close to half an hour, hoping for some sign of Finn Larson.

But all he had seen was Wilma Reed and Rob Turley, and there was something about the ease and freedom with which they moved about the compound that seemed to indicate they were alone. Occasionally, the woman's laughter carried up to Longarm. If the likes of Finn Larson was a guest of these two, such laughter would hardly be possible.

Wilma, astride a horse, appeared suddenly, coming from the direction of the barn. He watched her ride out of the compound, heading for the small herd of cattle grazing near the loop in the river. A moment before, Rob had been talking to her. Then he had disappeared in the direction of the small blacksmith shop alongside the stable. As the sound of Wilma's horse faded, Longarm could hear the steady clangor of Rob's hammer. Puffs of white smoke erupted from the blacksmith shop's stovepipe chimney.

And still there was no sign of Finn Larson.

With a sigh, Longarm guided his horse out from the pines and urged it to a fast gallop down the slope toward the ranch compound—his Winchester in one hand, his reins in the other. The jolting ride down the steep slope did nothing good to his aching head, but Longarm disregarded it and kept going. The black took a low wall with an easy jump. The pounding hooves brought Turley quickly out of the blacksmith shop.

Turley took one look and darted back into the shop, reappearing a second later with a sixgun. Galloping full tilt, Longarm took the reins in his teeth and raised the Winchester to his shoulder. As Turley got off a hasty shot, Longarm sighted quickly and squeezed the trigger.

Turley's revolver went flying. He grabbed his bleeding hand and dashed for the barn. Dismounting while his black was still in motion, Longarm flung himself after the man, crouching low as he ran. He did not slow down as he charged into the huge barn's dim interior.

He thought he saw movement at the rear of the barn, behind one of the stalls. Raising the Winchester, he squeezed off a quick shot. Too late, he heard the scuttle of hay over his head. Even as he tried to bring up his Winchester, Turley plunged down out of the hayloft, catching him in the back and driving him to his knees. He lost his grip on the rifle and it went skidding across the strawlittered floor.

Spinning around, Longarm saw Turley, a pitchfork clutched in his bloody hands, charging toward him. There was not time for Longarm to draw his sixgun. He ducked swiftly aside as Turley drove on past him, the tines slamming into the side of a horse stall. Turley tried to yank the pitchfork free. Longarm reached out and flung Turley to the ground. Then he pulled the pitchfork free and started for the man.

Turley scrambled to his feet and raced for Longarm's Winchester. As he snatched it up, Longarm flung the pitchfork aside and drew his .44. Turley was too panic-stricken to think clearly as he levered swiftly and fired. The bullet thudded into a post behind Longarm. Longarm went down on one knee, aimed carefully, and returned Turley's fire. The round caught the man high in the chest, slamming him back against the wall. Slowly, Turley sagged down the wall to the floor of the barn. Straightening cautiously, Longarm walked closer.

Rob Turley stared up at Longarm with unblinking eyes. Longarm reached down and took his Winchester back from the dead man.

As Longarm left the barn and started for his horse, he heard the rapid thunder of hooves. Glancing quickly to his right, he saw Wilma Reed riding full tilt toward him across the pasture. She had heard the shooting.

A rifle flashed in her hands as she brought it up and

squeezed off a shot. Longarm went down on one knee as the bullet sighed past his ear. He did not want to kill the woman. She had been a part of the Glendale train massacre, but he had long since decided against killing her. It was her man he wanted—and Finn Larson.

But she was deciding for him right now. That last shot had been a fine one. Another shot cracked from her rifle, and this time the ground exploded inches from his right foot as the bullet ricocheted through his legs. As Wilma's horse took the low fence bringing her into the compound, Longarm levered a fresh round into the Winchester's firing chamber, tracked her, and squeezed the trigger.

He worked the lever quickly once again, but it was not necessary. Wilma flung up both hands and went tumbling backward off her horse. She lay where she had fallen as her horse veered suddenly and galloped out through the compound's gate. Longarm got to his feet and walked over to the wounded woman.

She was lying on her back, her rifle on the ground behind her. There was a ragged hole in her chest, and blood from it was spreading rapidly, turning to crimson the white silk shirt she wore.

"Rob . . . ?" she whispered hoarsely, tears coursing down her cheeks. "Is Rob . . . ?"

Longarm went down on one knee beside her. "Yes," he said. "Rob's dead."

"And I am, too."

"I'm sorry. I didn't want to kill you. You left me no choice."

With some difficulty, she focused her eyes on his face. "I knew it was you. I know why you came for us. And for Finn, too. All those people on the train . . . terrible . . . I'm sorry." Suddenly she reached out with one hand, grabbed his coat, and pulled him closer. "Finn . . ." she managed.

"He's going after . . . Ellen Miller . . ."

Before Longarm could ask her anything more, her hand released his coat and her lifeless head fell back into the dust of the yard.

Ellen had spent most of the morning moving furniture and dishes from the dugout into the finished cabin. Laura and her father had taken the wagon over to Ron Walker's homestead to pick up what gear they had left there, while Doc Beaufort and Billy busied themselves inside the cabin, putting up cabinets over the sink.

Now she was outside the old dugout, hanging clothes out to dry on the clothesline Beaufort had strung. She was hurrying because it was almost time for the noon meal, and the doctor and Billy had just told her how hungry they were.

As she took the last sheet from the basket and draped it carefully over the line, she glanced beyond the clothesline and saw a Mexican rider cutting over from the river toward her. She took the clothespins from her mouth and pinned down both corners of the sheet, then looked again at the approaching rider.

He seemed to be coming directly for her. She could not see his face. It was lost in the shadow cast by the enormous brim of his sombrero. Nevertheless, something about the way he held himself on the horse troubled her vaguely. She reached down for the empty basket and started to walk across the grass toward the cabin entrance. At once she noticed how the Mexican shifted his horse's direction in order to intercept her.

She stopped and held her right hand up to shade her eyes as she peered intently at the face of the rider. He was closer now and she could see that the man's face was smooth, his mouth a thin, cruel line. And then he lifted his face enough for her to see his cold, icy blue eyes.

Dropping her basket, she turned and bolted for the cabin. Finn spurred his horse to a gallop, cutting her off.

Ellen spun around in terror. "Oh, Finn! Please!" she pleaded. "Leave me be! Please!"

"Leave you be?" Finn cried, grinning down at her. "I'm going to punish you—and then I'm going to take you back with me. There ain't no way you're going to get free of me this time!"

"I won't go back with you!" Ellen cried. "I won't!"

Finn lifted his head in laughter. "Who said you had any choice in the matter?"

He reached down and grabbed Ellen by the wrist; but when he tried to haul her up onto his horse, she yanked herself free and screamed. As she started to run toward the cabin, she saw Doc Beaufort bolt through the cabin doorway with a shotgun in his hand.

It was Billy, standing in the cabin's doorway, who had told the doctor of the Mexican's approach, and Ellen's scream brought Beaufort running. As he emerged from the cabin he saw Ellen, a few feet in front of the Mexican's horse, running toward him. The Mexican glanced past Ellen at Beaufort. His sombrero's brim effectively hid the rider's features, but as Ellen neared him, she shouted, "It's Finn! Finn Larson!"

"Get down, Ellen!" Beaufort yelled, rushing across the meadow toward them. "Get down! I can't shoot! You're in my line of fire!"

A rifle poked out of Finn's poncho. Beaufort saw it and tried to throw himself to one side. Finn's rifle barked, belching fire, and Beaufort felt something strike his thigh, knocking his leg out from under him. The rifle cracked again, and the second round struck him in the chest, its impact flipping him over onto his back.

He lost his shotgun when he fell. When he tried to roll over to retrieve it, he found that all the wires were down. He could not even move his fingers, let alone roll over. His breath was coming in sharp, painful gasps. Something terribly heavy was sitting on his chest. All he could do was stare up at the sky.

Hooves thundered close to his head, and the belly of a horse blocked out the sky as Finn rode over him. But the horse was careful and did not bring his hooves down on any part of him. Then Beaufort found himself staring up at Finn Larson.

The man was leaning out over his saddle, inspecting Beaufort as if he were a piece of butchered carcass that hadn't been hung up yet. A Colt materialized in his right hand. The sound of its hammer clicking back filled the universe. Beaufort closed his eyes and waited for the bullet's impact.

Instead, he heard Billy's cry and a shrill scream of outrage from Ellen. Opening his eyes, he saw Billy and Ellen pulling the startled Finn from his horse. As Finn tumbled out of his saddle to the ground, he dropped his sixgun. But he was back on his feet in an instant, and with a brutal kick sent Billy sprawling to the ground.

Then he grabbed Ellen, snatched his Colt out of the grass, and struck her viciously across the face with it. It snuffed out her cries instantly as she sagged forward into his arms.

In an agony of despair because he could not go to Ellen's aid, Beaufort tried to rouse himself. But the enormous, crushing heaviness in his chest seemed to have increased tenfold.

Draping Ellen's limp body over his pommel, Finn turned to look down at Beaufort. "If you can hear me, Doc, tell Longarm I'll be waiting for him."

Then he swung into his saddle and rode off.

Chapter 10

As soon as Longarm came in sight of the Millers' new cabin the next morning, he knew he was too late. Bill Miller and Laura were standing in the doorway as he rode up and they remained there while he dismounted. Only when he neared the cabin did Miller leave his daughter and come out to meet him. Looking past Bill Miller at Laura's pale, wan face, Longarm learned much that he did not want to know.

"Finn's been here, right?" Longarm said.

Miller nodded dully. "He took Ellen back with him."

"She's alive, then?"

"Just barely. Billy said Finn beat her fearfully before he rode off with her. Said he draped her over his saddle. Billy also said Finn told Doc Beaufort he'd be waiting for you. The kid was hurt pretty bad himself. Finn kicked him in the stomach."

"Will he be all right?"

"I think so. He's starting to eat again."

Longarm took a quick look at Laura, then glanced back at Miller. "Where's Beaufort?"

Miller turned slightly and pointed to the river. "He's over there, six feet under. We buried him on a spot overlooking the river yesterday."

"I think I'll take a walk over there."

The man nodded. "When you come back we'll have some grub for you. And a bed to sleep on. You look pretty worn around the edges."

Longarm nodded, left his horse with Miller, and walked over in the direction he had indicated.

The sun was high when Longarm reached the Deer River range the next day. He rode straight for the pines, then followed the trail to the ridge leading to Finn's valley. He was within half a mile of the spot where Finn had forced Cal Swinnerton off the trail when he caught the glint of sunlight on a gunbarrel among the rocks ahead of him.

He pulled up at once and dismounted, cursing himself for his stupidity. Finn was up there on the trail, waiting for him. Where would he find a better spot than that same narrow trail where he had finished off Cal Swinnerton?

Swiftly Longarm turned his horse about and led it back down the trail. Once he was certain he was far enough away so that the black's galloping hooves would not carry to Finn, he spurred the animal down the trail. As soon as he came out in the pines, he galloped full-tilt toward the River and then followed it into the mountains.

When he came to the spot where he had noticed the vultures circling, he dismounted and found once again the passage that took him through the mountain wall. Climbing swiftly through it, he moved on past the waterfall and into the narrow defile where only the polished bones of Cal Swinnerton remained. Moving back out of the defile, he spied once again the trail he had taken to the ridge above.

He had carried no rifle on that earlier climb, he realized.

This time, if he wanted to keep the rifle with him, he would find the going considerably more difficult. But there was no question that, if he made it, he would catch Finn totally by surprise.

Longarm started up.

A hundred or so feet up the side of the wall, he found himself pulling his straining body along a sheer plane of rock toward a niche cut out of the rockface above it. As he reached the niche and pulled himself into it, the spur of rock he used for a handhold suddenly groaned and, spewing tiny pebbles out ahead of it, wrenched itself free and went tumbling down the steep slope. By the time it had gone halfway, it had already collected enough debris and loose gravel to turn it into a small but quite noisy avalanche.

It was the noise that worried him—that could kill him. He flattened himself well into the niche and waited for any sign that Finn, crouching on the trail above, had heard the avalanche. Longarm did not have long to wait. He heard an aborted, strangled cry from Ellen as she attempted to call out a warning to him. Soon thereafter, a rifle cracked, the bullet from it striking a boulder just above Longarm's head before it ricocheted with an ear-splitting whine off into the canyon.

Another shot followed, and then another. But all the bullets went screaming off covering rock. Longarm remained perfectly still, hugging his Winchester to him. It was obvious that Finn could not see him. His target practice was just a way of satisfying himself that Longarm was not coming up at him from that flank. A few more shots followed the first volley, then the firing ceased.

Longarm waited nearly a quarter of an hour before resuming his climb. He moved now with infinite care, testing each handhold carefully before calling upon it to support his full weight. He did not so much climb as insinuate

163

himself up the wall of rock. He was like an enormous worm, seeking every ridge, taking advantage of each outcropping of rock for cover, then slithering around it, pushing his Winchester silently ahead of him as if it were a single, menacing feeler.

He was within sight of the trail when he caught the chink of spurs and heard Finn's sullen voice snap something at Ellen. Longarm heard her snarl back at him just as readily. The exchange was followed by a slap that echoed loudly in this rocky wasteland.

From what little Longarm heard, he judged that Finn was becoming impatient, tired of stationing himself on the trail. Soon, perhaps, the man might decide it would be best for him to retreat to his valley, to wait for Longarm there.

Longarm did not want that to happen.

Looking up at that portion of the slope he had yet to climb, however, Longarm realized he had a problem. The incline from his present position to the top was not as steep as that which he had already negotiated. It was almost a forty-five-degree angle. It was not the incline that was the problem, however. As he made this final dash to the trail above him, he would be moving across open rock and would for a considerable time be fully exposed.

But he would have to chance it, he realized. Grabbing his Winchester, he left the cover of the boulder he was crouching behind and started to scramble up the rock face. He had removed his spurs, and his passage across the rock was reasonably quiet, but in the awesome silence of the place, the sound of his boots striking its smooth surface began to echo significantly.

Finn turned around swiftly. He could hear someone running along the trail, yet he saw nothing. There was no one there. Ellen was also turning at the sound.

At that moment Longarm—rifle in hand—exploded into view from below the trail.

Finn had been right. There *had* been someone climbing up that cliff face. Even as this astounding thought raced through his mind, his rifle was spitting a rapid fusillade of bullets at Longarm. But it was already too late, as the lawman dove swiftly for cover behind a mess of boulders.

Nor was Longarm's rifle quiet, either. Only his weapon was more accurate as it sent a bullet tearing into Finn's sombrero, knocking it off his head so that it hung down his back by the chin strap. Another bullet struck the wall by his head, sending tiny shards of stone into his eyes. Finn ducked his head down and began to dig them out.

Another round sang past his bowed head. Without thinking about it any further, Finn ducked up a small slope, scrambling for the protection of a large boulder. But Longarm followed him relentlessly and Finn now felt himself at a distinct disadvantage. It was impossible for him to climb for cover and shoot at the same time.

As Longarm's fire whined past his buttocks, Finn dropped his rifle and, using both hands, hauled himself out of sight of the trail and up behind the boulder. Crouching low, he took out his sixgun and peered around the base of the rock. Longarm was just below him, taking deliberate aim. As Finn looked out, the rifle bucked. Finn pulled himself back behind the boulder as the bullet whined past.

Finn looked around him. He was trapped! The slope went no higher. And Ellen was down there now with that son-ofabitch. Jesus! And he was supposed to have been waiting to bushwhack Longarm! What the hell had gone wrong this time? He leaned his back wearily against the boulder and glared up at the sun, which glared right back down at him out of a cloudless sky. Sweat was pouring off him. He checked to make sure his gun was fully loaded.

But what the hell difference did that make? Every time he poked his head out, he'd be giving Longarm a clear shot. He had to think of something.

On the trail below, Longarm was lying flat behind a slab of rock, his rifle sighted on the boulder behind which Finn was still crouching. One of the bullets Finn had sent at him during that first, furious fusillade had caught him in the right shoulder. The resulting wound had been superficial, and was no longer bleeding. Longarm was able to hold his rifle perfectly steady while he waited for Finn to show his face again.

Ellen joined him. "You're hurt!" she cried. "Your shoulder. It's bleeding!"

"The bullet's gone clear through. It's nothing. And you'd better get back."

Obediently, Ellen moved away, so that she was no longer in sight of the boulder. Longarm began to wonder what Finn's next move would be.

Then, as if in answer, Finn called out, "Longarm!"

"What do you want, Finn?"

"You got me trapped, good and proper. I give up. I'm going to throw down my sixgun and come out. You can take me in. I ain't goin' to fight you no more."

As he spoke, Finn stepped coolly out from behind the boulder, holding his sixgun by the barrel. Keeping his rifle trained on the man, Longarm rose carefully to his feet.

"Toss the gun away, Finn," Longarm told him.

Finn threw the gun onto the ledge beside Longarm, who promptly kicked it over the edge of the trail. It made a distant, metallic echo as it slammed to pieces on the rocks below. Finn kept coming until he was on the trail facing Longarm, his eyes shifting warily from Longarm to Ellen.

Finn smiled. "Sure looks like you got me, lawman," he said resignedly, almost cheerfully.

"Longarm," said Ellen fearfully, "I don't like it. He's up to something."

Finn laughed. "Why, Ellen! Why are you so nervous about ol' Finn? Longarm's got him all hung up to dry."

Longarm glanced up the trail at Ellen, intending to ask her to get Finn's horse. That one moment of inattention was all Finn had been waiting for. Pulling a huge Bowie knife out of his shirt, he lunged at Longarm.

Longarm started to bring his rifle up, but before he could, Finn was on him, the knife slicing down wickedly. Dropping his rifle, Longarm slipped to one side. The knife flashed down, passing inches from his shoulder. Longarm grabbed Finn's wrist with both hands, then twisted. With a shrill scream of agony, Finn dropped the knife. Longarm kicked it off the trail, then flung Finn backward, drawing his sixgun as he did so.

"Hold it right there, Finn," Longarm told him. "Don't give me one more excuse to pull this trigger—because that's just what I'm looking for."

Picking up Longarm's rifle, Ellen moved quickly up beside him. "Let me kill the sonofabitch," she said. "Let me do it, Longarm!"

Startled, Longarm glanced at Ellen. Her eyes were fierce with loathing. Sobered by the sight, Longarm felt his own fury subside somewhat. Holstering his revolver, he reached for the Winchester. But Ellen stepped quickly away from him and aimed the rifle at Finn.

Finn was staring at Ellen. He glanced nervously at Longarm. For the first time, he looked worried. "She's crazy!" he cried. "You ain't gonna let her do this, Longarm!"

"He's not going to be able to stop me, Finn," Ellen said, swiftly levering a fresh cartridge into the firing chamber.

With a cry, Finn leaped for Ellen. Longarm reached out to grab him. Ducking away from Longarm, Finn did not watch where he placed his feet. He slipped. With a look of pure horror on his face, Finn glanced down and saw his feet sliding on loose gravel. He reached out to grab hold of something, anything, to keep himself from going over, but he was too close to the edge.

He came down hard on one knee, his feet well out over the edge. Grabbing desperately at a small shrub, he succeeded only in pulling it out of the ground, roots and all.

With a terrified scream, he vanished over the edge.

His scream was cut off abruptly. Longarm peered over the edge. Finn was lying on his back on a narrow ledge less than twenty yards below, staring up at them both. A thin trickle of blood was running from one corner of his mouth.

"I can't move!" he called up to them. "My back! It's broke! I landed on something!"

"Another filthy trick," Ellen said.

"I don't think so. Where's his horse?"

"Back down the trail."

"Bring it here, and make sure he has a lariat. I'll lower it to him and let the horse pull him up."

"No! Leave him be! Let him rot on that ledge!"

Longarm looked at her. "I said get the horse!"

She returned a few minutes later with Finn's horse. His lariat was looped over the saddlehorn. Longarm let it down to Finn. The man had not moved a muscle while Longarm waited for Ellen to return with his horse. The end of the rope nudged Finn on the chest, but he made no attempt to reach up and grab it.

"I told you," Finn gasped. "I can't move! My back's broke. You sonofabitch! You done it to me! Both of you! I can't move!"

Longarm pulled up the rope and looked around for something he could tie it to so he could lower himself to the ledge. But there was nothing close enough. Then he looked at the horse. Perhaps he could tie the rope to the saddlehorn. But he didn't trust the horse, not on this narrow, treacherous trail. There was too much gravel.

Suddenly a shadow passed over him. Ellen glanced quickly up and shaded her eyes to watch a large buzzard drifting not too far overhead. Longarm glanced up at it also. It would be the first of many that would soon begin to visit the ledge below them, unless they could somehow manage to pull Finn up.

"Good!" Ellen said softly.

Longarm knew what she was thinking. Vultures did not drop upon carrion because they smelled death, but because they detected a carcass that did not move, a body that lay in the hot sun without protection or movement for long periods of time. They would eventually alight on Finn's ledge. Finn would scream, but he would not be able to move. After a while the birds would ignore his screams and begin to feed—and while Finn still lived, their foul beaks would tear into his warm flesh.

Longarm reached out and took his Winchester from Ellen.

When she saw what he intended to do, she cried, "No! Let him be! It's what the sonofabitch deserves! Let the buzzards pick him apart!"

"No, Ellen. It's what you want now—but not later, when you think back on it."

Longarm fitted the stock to his shoulder and took careful aim at Finn's face.

"Go ahead, you bastard!" Finn cried. "I'll see you in hell! That's a promise!"

Sighting quickly, Longarm squeezed the trigger. The bullet struck Finn's face like an invisible boot, stamping one side of it into the ledge. Longarm fired a second time, to make sure.

He turned away. Ellen was weeping silently, her face averted. Longarm glanced skyward. Another vulture had joined the first.

Chapter 11

Longarm entered the room, a smile on his face, and handed the telegram to the curious Cynthia. She took it from him and read it swiftly.

> GET BACK HERE STOP YOU ARE STILL ON PAYROLL STOP YOU WERE ON EXTENDED LEAVE STOP YOU HEARD ME STOP GET BACK HERE STOP VAIL

Cynthia looked up at Longarm, an impish grin on her face. "I think he wants you to get back to Denver as soon as you can. I think he misses you."

"That's just what I thought, too. It's nice to be wanted. I answered the telegram, told him I'd need another week to recover. Told him I fell from a horse and reinjured my skull."

"So you think he'll believe it?" she asked, putting both arms around his neck and pulling him as close to her as he could get.

He smiled, then kissed her on the lips. "I think he will."

"How much time does that give us?"

"Another couple of days, anyway."

"Let's make the most of them, Longarm."

"I intend to," he said, kissing her, then abruptly lifting her in his arms and carrying her to the bed.

It was night. Longarm was standing at the window, looking down at the streets of Cody. Cynthia was asleep on the bed behind him. The streets were still busy with people, and from this distance all of them looked perfectly harmless, peaceful even. There was so little in a man's or a woman's face, he realized, to give a clue as to what the soul contained. Finn Larson had been a handsome man. Clean-shaven, fair complexion, blond hair, blue eyes. Yet beneath that mild exterior had beat a heart as black as coal.

And Ellen. After what she had been through, Longarm would have guessed that by this time she would have been simply unable to function. All during the ride back to her father's place after Finn's death, he had feared for her sanity. She alternately laughed and cried. Her mind had seemed perched on the brink. That last terrible assault on her by Finn had almost destroyed her. For a while Longarm thought that it had.

Yet now, according to what Cynthia had told him, she was a tower of strength. It was she who had taken Laura in hand and helped to heal the terrible wound the death of Beaufort had caused the girl who had loved him.

And Lemuel T. Beaufort. He was a doctor who had the look of death about him, a man dying of a disease that had defeated and would continue to defeat the best physicians in the world. Yet for a while he prospered on that flat as he helped Bill Miller establish his spread. To his and everyone else's amazement, this cynical, hard-bitten physician

172

had seemed on the verge of a new, healthy life—and then he had given up that promise and his life to save a woman he barely knew.

And what about himself? Had he gone too far, as Ellen had suggested earlier? Had he turned himself into judge, jury, and executioner? Was that why he had holed up in this town, refusing to return to Denver or even to wire Billy Vail? Had he gone bad, finally?

Cynthia stirred behind him. He turned. She was sitting up in the bed, stretching deliciously. Her presence here in Cody with him had been her gift, her way of saying thank you, she told him when she got off the stage the day before and stepped into his waiting arms. It was she who had insisted he wire Vail.

"Come here," she said, patting the bed beside her. "You've been brooding again. I can tell."

"You're right," he said, sitting down beside her. "Make me stop."

"That's just what I'm going to do. And do you know what else I'm going to do?"

"No, what?"

"I have decided. I'm going to visit Denver with you for a while. I will cause a mild scandal, then come back and find myself a good solid farmer and give him plenty of healthy sons." She smiled at him and leaned her head against her chest. "How does that sound?"

"Sounds very good. I wish I were a young farmer."

She pushed him away and looked deep into his eyes. "No, you don't, Mr. Custis Long. You are a lawman. Justice is your calling. And that is what you gave us in Deer River. Don't you ever forget that."

He was astonished at her words, and pleased as well. He kissed her on the tip of her nose. "I won't," he said.

"That's fine. Now let's make love again—before we go

down for supper—and maybe have some champagne?"

"It's a deal," he assured her, bearing her gently down beneath him, his lips finding the soft flesh just behind her ears. She murmured happily and drew her arms more tightly about him.

Watch for

LONGARM IN THE BADLANDS

forty-seventh novel in the bold
LONGARM series from Jove

coming in September!

SPECIAL PREVIEW

COMING IN AUGUST!!!

In the most exciting, biggest Longarm novel
ever, LONGARM AND THE LONE STAR
LEGEND, Longarm meets the hot new western
duo of Jessica Starbuck and Ki, soon to appear
in their own Jove western series.

A shape detached itself from the shadows beneath the veranda to reveal itself as a huge, hulking man, standing at least as tall as Longarm, but outweighing the Deputy by at least twenty pounds. None of that extra weight looked like fat, either. He was dressed in a suit, complete with a string tie in place down the front of his grimy white shirt. "Hold it, boy!" the man snapped out at the young wrangler, countermanding Jessica's orders. "Just who is it staying with us, Miss Jessie?"

"This doesn't concern you, Higgins," Jessica said.

"As foreman of this here outfit, I guess it'll be me who decides what concerns me or not... With all due respect, Miss Jessie." He grinned, his smile yellow-toothed and resembling that of a grizzly just before it cracks open a honey-sweet beehive. He ambled over to Longarm's horse, patting its flanks as he looked the gelding over. "Fine animal. Don't often see a hand with his own mount." He turned to stare at Longarm. "You signing on as a hand, boy?"

"I'm signing on to dig your grave if you call me 'boy'

again," Longarm told him. There was the sound of guffaws swiftly choked off. Four more men stepped out from the interior darkness of the veranda to lean against the railing.

Longarm looked them over. They were wearing expensive Stetsons and shiny Justin boots, though the rest of their clothes were broken down and dusty. Their gunbelts were cracked and scuffed, cinched tightly about their waists. Longarm didn't have to examine their weapons to know that they'd be single-action weapons, working hands' weapons—not the kind of guns that man-killers carried. They were a wolf pack following their big bad he-wolf, Higgins. They could be troublesome when drunk, all of them against one man in the dark, but they were nothing but wind when stared down in broad daylight.

Higgins, however, glancing back at them, did not appear sorry to see them. "You son of a bitch," he said to Longarm.

"Easy, boss," one of the men on the veranda warned.

"Shut up, Ray," Higgins glowered back over his shoulder. He looked back at Longarm. "I called you a son of a bitch."

"Now that ain't much better than 'boy,'" Longarm drawled. "Try again, else I'll have to fetch me a shovel."

Higgins flushed red. He whipped off his Stetson to wipe at the sweat dewing his brow. He was horse-shoe bald. His hatband had pressed a red ridge across his ivory pate. "You get your horse," he snarled, "and ride off this spread."

"Whether I stay or go is up to Jessica," Longarm explained. "That's *Miss Jessie* to you," he added.

Higgins unbuttoned his suit jacket.

"Easy, old son," Longarm cautioned. "I can see you're carrying your gun in a shoulder rig. You ought to realize there's damn little chance you can outdraw me."

Higgins, his hand hovering in midair, seemed to think that what Longarm had said was good advice.

178

"This has gone far enough, Higgins," Jessica fumed. "Now get back to work."

"Your daddy made me foreman, and it's my job to take care of you," Higgins argued.

"Your job is to take care of this spread, period," Jessica said.

"Now don't go getting all riled, Miss Jessie." Higgins winked slyly. "You know I only got your best interests at heart."

More men have their eyes on this filly than Texas has cows, Longarm thought to himself. Plain as day, Higgins saw himself as Jessica's beau, regardless of how Jessica saw it.

"Just get back to work," Jessie said disgustedly.

"First I'll take his gun," Higgins replied, pointing at Longarm. "I'm doing it for you, Miss Jessie. With your daddy being shot dead and all, we can't have no strangers being around you armed."

"Higgins, I'm warning you—" Jessica began, but Higgins waved her aside as he strode down the steps of the veranda.

"Hush now, girl. Your daddy would want me to do this." He advanced upon Longarm, his hand outstretched. "Give me your gun, boy. Else you'll have to outshoot me *and* the four behind me."

Longarm prepared himself for trouble, but just then Ki glided between the deputy and the burly foreman.

"Miss Jessica has given you an order, Higgins," the unarmed man said in his soft voice.

"Get out of my way!"

Ki was now less than a yard away from the foreman. He seemed dwarfed by Higgins's hulking form. "You are not being polite to our guest, Higgins."

"Now that Mr. Starbuck is dead, maybe there's no room

179

for you on this spread," Higgins snarled. "What do you think, boys?" he called over his shoulder.

"Get rid of him, boss," one of the men called.

"Bust his hole," another chortled.

"That tears it." Higgins grinned. "Run along, China-man—"

Before he could say another word, Ki struck with a round-house kick. His torso bent sideways as his leg came around straight and true, his foot catching Higgins beneath the chin.

The foreman rose about six inches in the air, and then fell, to land hard on his butt. By then, Ki was back in a relaxed, standing position. The whole kick and return had taken less time than a rattlesnake takes to strike.

"I am of Japanese ancestry, not Chinese, Higgins," Ki said, staring down at the foreman. "But you needn't grovel in the dirt. Merely apologize."

Higgins lumbered to his feet. He was swearing and spit-ting in rage. He tugged out from beneath his jacket a blue-steel Peacemaker. But before he could even thumb back the hammer on the single-action weapon, Ki moved in fast. He swatted Higgins's gun with the edge of his right hand. The Peacemaker went flying off in the direction of the Texas Panhandle as Higgins yelped in surprise and clasped his wrist.

"Shoot the yellow chink!" Higgins shouted in frustration to his men.

Longarm quickly moved toward the veranda, drawing his Colt as he did so. "Let's all stay out of this, boys. What do you say?"

The four men stared at Longarm's Colt. They noticed that its barrel had been cut down to five inches, and that it lacked a front sight. They looked at the cross-draw rig, and then back at the gun trained rock-steady upon them. "He's a gunslick, we can't do nothing!" one of them said.

Gradually they lifted their hands toward the pitched roof of the veranda.

"Then I'll kill you myself, chink. With my bare hands," Higgins huffed, now truly resembling a grizzly. He moved warily around Ki, who stood motionless, not even bothering to turn as Higgins attacked from behind.

As the foreman looped both brawny arms around Ki's neck, the smaller man thrust his elbow into the other's solar plexus. Higgins gasped in pain, his arms going limp, now encompassing nothing but thin air. Ki slammed his elbow into Higgins's ribs, and the foreman staggered like a pole-axed steer. Ki swept Higgins's boots out from under the heavy man, using only his own bare foot, but that foot was like a straw broom sweeping away litter. Higgins landed on his knees, and then toppled all the way to the ground. He rolled over onto his back, his breath coming in agonized rasps as he clutched at his chest and side.

Light as a feather, Ki knelt beside him. With one hand he tilted Higgins's chin to expose the foreman's throat. "If I struck here," he said, his finger gently tracing Higgins's Adam's apple, "you would choke to death on your own crushed throat."

"Please..." Higgins gasped, his eyes rolling white. Ki's rigid grip had arced his neck back at an impossible angle. Higgins resembled—in more ways than one—a chicken with its neck stretched across the chopping block.

"Or here," Ki continued, ignoring Higgins's plea. He touched the foreman's nose. "If I struck here, shards of bone would drive themselves into your pig's brain. Your life would bleed out of your ears into the dust—"

"Ki," Jessica called. "Don't. Let him go."

After a moment, Ki smiled and nodded. "Higgins, am I Chinese?"

"No..."

"What am I, Higgins?"

"Japanese . . ." the foreman gurgled, and then moaned.

"Half Japanese," Ki remarked. "But close enough, Higgins, close enough."

12-3-06
9-7-09

Bestselling Books for Today's Reader — From Jove!

___ **THE AMERICANS**   05432-1/$2.95
     John Jakes

___ **BURIED BLOSSOMS**   05153-5/$2.95
     Stephen Lewis

___ **FIFTH JADE OF HEAVEN**   04628-0/$2.95
     Marilyn Granbeck

___ **HAND-ME-DOWNS**   06425-4/$2.95
     Rhea Kohan

___ **NIGHTWING**   06241-7/$2.95
     Martin Cruz Smith

___ **SHIKE: TIME OF THE DRAGONS**   06586-2/$3.25
     (Book 1) Robert Shea

___ **SHIKE: LAST OF THE ZINJA**   06587-0/$3.25
     (Book 2) Robert Shea

___ **A SHARE OF EARTH AND GLORY**   04756-2/$3.50
     Katherine Giles

___ **THE WOMEN'S ROOM**   05933-1/$3.50
     Marilyn French

___ **YELLOW ROSE**   05557-3/$3.50
     Shana Carrol

Available at your local bookstore or return this form to:

J **JOVE/BOOK MAILING SERVICE**
P.O. Box 690, Rockville Center, N.Y. 11570

Please enclose 75¢ for postage and handling for one book, 25¢ each add'l. book ($1.50 max.). No cash, CODs or stamps. Total amount enclosed: $ _____ in check or money order.

NAME _____

ADDRESS _____

CITY _____ STATE/ZIP _____

Allow six weeks for delivery.   **SK 23**